# Brennen: Encouraged to Intercede

## The Barnabas Chronicles
## Book 9

By

Ronna M. Bacon

ISBN 978-1-989699-42-3

Ephesians 6

18 And pray in the Spirit on all occasions with all kinds of prayers and requests. With this in mind, be alert and always keep on praying for all the Lord's people.

Ezekiel 22
30 I looked for someone among them who would build up the wall and stand before me in the gap on behalf of the land so I would not have to destroy it, but I found no one.

# Table of Contents

# Chapter 1

Standing in front of the window in the living room of the small, rough-framed cabin that she called home, Jaxcy Dering wrapped her hands around the brown stoneware mug of tea she held, trying to control the shivers running through her. It was late spring and damp in the province she lived in, that of Newfoundland and Labrador. A late spring snowstorm was blanketing the ground in white, making it difficult for her to see the towering pine trees that surrounded her home. She finally turned to set her mug down on a pine table near her favourite chair, to reach for a log to drop into the fireplace, and then moved to the kitchen to replenish the wood in that stove. Living out in the country as she did, she didn't have electricity. It was too expensive to bring in.

A sound from the bedroom had her heading that way, a puzzled look crossing her face that settled into the deep gray eyes that almost seemed too large for her face. She pulled at the black hair she had in a braid, uncertainty in her very movements. She sighed once more. This is it, isn't it, Lord? I have to face the music as Mom would have said. How do I do just that?

Jaxcy paused in the bedroom doorway, a smile crossing her face as she watched her blue merle Shetland Sheepdog curled up tight to the form lying there. He had refused to leave the man, claiming him as his own.

"Kerry, you do need to move, you know? You can't stay there all day." Jaxcy moved quietly around the room, tidying an already tidy room, delaying the inevitable, she thought. She finally turned to the bed, to slip to a seating position on it, a hand reaching out to lay on the man's forehead, finding it cool once more.

His head tossing restlessly, the man's eyes flickered open and closed, finally remaining open. He licked at his dry lips, sipping gratefully at the mug of water that Jaxcy held up to his mouth. He swallowed hard, before he focused on her, a frown momentarily crossing his face.

"Where am I?"

"You're in my home." Jaxcy watched him closely. "How are you feeling?"

"Sore. What did I do?"

"What did you do? Let's see. You apparently arrived here on the Rock a week ago, got yourself in trouble somehow, were beaten up, and taken in by me." She stared across the room. "What do you remember?" When he didn't reply, she looked back at him, finding his hazel eyes focused on her. "I asked, what do you remember?"

"Not a lot. I remember you. You helped me." His hand laid gently on her arm. "Thank you."

Jaxcy shrugged. "I had to. They wouldn't have stopped, you know. They are the troublemakers in town, but they shouldn't have targeted you. You're a stranger in town. That much we determined."

"Why am I here?" His head moved restlessly. "This isn't a hospital room."

"No, it's not. You were there for a day or so before I brought you home." She looked down at her hands, studying them. "You had nowhere else to go."

The man shifted his position, his eyes on her, before he scrubbed a hand at his face, frowning. "I have no whiskers."

"No, you don't. You insisted on being shaved every day. You didn't ask for much more than that. I couldn't trim your hair." She lightly touched the dark auburn waves. "I tried, but you refused."

"I did? That's not like me." He sighed. "I need to introduce myself. I'm Brennen Connolly." Brennen watched as her faced tightened momentarily before his hand rested on the dog laying with his head on his chest. "Who is this?"

"That's Kerry. He has claimed you. I have had trouble getting him to leave you. You need to rest, Brennen. The town doctor was to be out today, but it's snowing too hard."

"Snowing? It's spring!"

"I know it is. This is what happens here. It snows in the spring." She rose, walking away from him, not answering his call for her to come back, that he needed to know her name.

Brennen sighed, his eyes drifting closed as he slept. Jaxcy returned to watch him, to reach and tuck his hands back under the covers, her finger lightly resting on the wedding band he wore before she turned

—

and almost ran from the room, tears blinding her briefly.

Lord, what did I do? What did I do? Mom and Dad would be shocked, horrified, I think. I know, Lord. You didn't say no, did You? I had to, Lord. I just had to. He had no one.

Jaxcy huddled down on the rickety couch in her living room, reaching for the threadbare blanket to wrap herself in, her eyes on her hands, studying the matching wedding band on her finger. She had had no choice, she thought. She sat for hours like that, before she heard a shuffling sound and jumped as Brennen sank down beside her, dressed in the clothes that she had washed and left on a chair, not knowing when or if he would ever use them again.

"You shouldn't be up." She shoved back the blanket wrapped around her, ready to rise before his hand rested on her arm.

"Please? Talk to me? I don't understand." He stared at his hand. "I'm not married. I don't understand why I'm wearing a wedding ring."

Jaxcy sighed and then swallowed hard. I guess the time of reckoning is here, isn't it, Lord? How do I explain to this man, this stranger, that we are truly married?

"You are. We had no choice. There is a law in this village or town or whatever you want to call it. Unless strangers have a reason to be here, they have to leave. If they don't, then they are jailed. The only way around it is if they marry someone local. It doesn't matter if they are only in town for a day or longer. The authorities here are a law to themselves. They have driven so many young people away. I would have left if I could have." She blinked rapidly.

"But I don't understand. Why am I here? If I'm married, where is my wife?" He frowned as he saw the devastation crossing her face. "Can you tell me what is the matter?"

Jaxcy sighed. "I guess I have to tell you who I am. You were alert enough that we could question you, to find out a personal history on you, enough that we could save you. The minister in town, an old man by the name of Brown, helped us." She blinked rapidly against the tears that she was refusing to shed. "I am Jaxcy Joelyn Dering Connolly. I am your wife." She was on her feet, running across the room, reaching for her jacket, shoving her feet into her boots before she wrenched open the door and was through it, the door swinging shut behind her.

Brennen stood, a hand on the top of his head, as he stared after her, shock on his face. What did I do, Lord? What did I do? I was asked to come to this village. I know I talked to Barnabas and Breck about it and they agreed I needed to. There was someone here who had requested that I come. But, who was that? It doesn't sound as if I made that contact.

He sank back on the couch, Kerry jumping up beside him, a paw on his leg, before Brennen's hand rubbed at the dog's head.

"Well, boy, what do we do now? I'm a husband and have no idea of how to be just that. I don't remember the ceremony and that's not fair to her.

Lord? Where do I go from here? Please, Lord? I need help. I am definitely in over my head." He finally rose, heading for the kitchen, stopping to replenish the logs in the fireplace, finding the room chilling.

Brennen searched the kitchen, finding only tea and no coffee. He wasn't a tea drinker, he thought, but it looked as if he had no choice. He searched for food, finding a loaf of homemade bread and butter, and then searching for meat or something he could use for sandwiches. He was hard at work making a meal when the door opened and a flurry of snowflakes blew in with the cold wind. He shivered before he turned, finding Jaxcy not looking at him.

"Jaxcy? Thank you. We will talk, but first, have you eaten?"

"No, I haven't. I haven't had much of an appetite. Are you sure you want that sandwich? I have broth as well." She moved past him to reach into the fridge or icebox, he thought, to retrieve the container of broth and then dump it into a pot to heat, sliding it onto the stove, rattling around it as she did so.

"Let's have that, shall we, or do you want the tea that you have in the cupboard?" Brennen's words were careful as he worked away, watching Jaxcy as he did so. "Where do you normally eat?" He eyed the small table, seeing the makeshift repairs to it. How has she ever lived, Lord? This place is not where she should be. That much I can see. She's a princess, a princess in denim and flannel, and she's my princess. I need to change all this. He didn't stop to think why he muttered that to himself. He didn't realize that Jaxcy had already claimed his heart.

"I usually eat in front of the fireplace. Especially in the cold weather." She took her plate and mug of broth with a quiet word of thanks before leading the way back across the long room that held both the kitchen and living room.

"We'll talk, Jaxcy. First, we eat. Then, we pray. Then, we'll talk."

Jaxcy looked at him in surprise and then relief. A believer, she thought. Thank you, Lord. It could have been so much worse.

Brennen finally rose, gathering their dishes, carrying them through to stack them tidily in the sink, a frown on his face as he realized she didn't have running water. He turned, reaching for the tray he had readied, setting the teapot on it, and then returning to the living room, to set the tray on the table in front of them. He reached out his hand, palm up, waiting for her to respond, feeling her tentative touch as she finally took his hand.

He prayed, not sure afterward what it was that he had prayed, but knowing that something he had said reached to her. He felt her fingers relaxing from their tenseness, tightening slightly on his. He waited after he had finished, his eyes on the floor, before he looked up, to find her studying him.

"Just who are you, Brennen?" Jaxcy was curious, to know about the man that she had married.

"I work as an illustrator for children's books. But there is more to that than what it implies. I am employed by The Barnabas Foundation, who pays my wages, allowing me to work for my employer. This allows the employer to hire on others as he needs to without worrying about cash. I am an orphan, raised in foster care in Labrador. Barnabas Carey, the chairman of the Barnabas Foundation, found me and offered me work. I accepted. There is something interesting about all this. He has hired twelve of us, plus one other man. The twelve of us are orphans, coming from a different province or territory, but we all share the same initial. He said God told him to do that. Part of the creed of the Foundation is to be encouragers, based on Barnabas of the Bible."

"So it is named for him as well as your friend?" Jaxcy watched as he nodded. "I see. That's interesting. But it doesn't explain why you are here."

"That is the strange part. I was contacted and asked to come here. I talked it over with both Barnabas and Breck, prayed about it, and then flew here. I was to contact a J.J. Dering." He paused, his eyes suddenly on her. "That's you!"

"Those are my initials, but I didn't contact you." Her eyes slid closed. "It had to be Johnny. He's the minister. He's old enough to be my grandfather. He knew what I was facing."

"And that would be?" Brennen reached for her hands, rubbing his fingers along hers, trying to warm hers.

"I have been threatened. We don't know why. We can't find the ones behind it. But the toughs who beat you up are employed by someone. It really seemed as if they were watching for you."

"And why would they be doing that?"

Jaxcy shrugged. "We don't know. I don't have money." Her hand waved in the air around her. "I'm not rich." She paled. "I forgot. How could I forget?"

"What did you forget? Jaxcy? What did you forget?"

She scrambled from the couch, running towards a desk in the corner of the room, yanking open the drawers and rifling through the papers inside, finally pulling out a long envelope. She walked back slowly towards him, her face pale, before she sank back beside him, handing it to him.

"What is this?" At her nod, he slid out the paperwork inside and read it. "Jaxcy? Do you know what this is?" She shook her head, her eyes not leaving his face. "Jaxcy. This is a deed to the property and for stocks and bonds that come to you when you turn twenty-eight." He looked up at a sound from her. "Jaxcy? When are you twenty-eight?"

"Yesterday. It was yesterday. But, what does this mean?"

"It means that you have come into a certain amount of wealth. How much, I can't tell from this. We need to talk to someone." He studied the deed, and his face paled. "Jaxcy, have you ever traveled to Ontario?"

"No, I have never been outside of this village. Why?"

"Because this is property near where I live. It borders the Foundation property. We need to head back there."

"We do? But how? And who?"

Brennen's face grew grim as he read through an attached letter. "It names the person here. I know him. He is brutal. He would kill you to get his hands on this. And it says that if you are not married by the time you reach that age, the property will revert to a trust, which then turns over to this man. Oh, Jaxcy. Thank God I was here."

# Chapter 2

Brennen paced the cabin the next morning, waiting for Jaxcy to return from outdoors. He smiled at how she had had to persuade Kerry that he really needed to go outside, finally just picking up the dog and walking away, muttering to herself as she did so. He wasn't quite sure if he had heard her right, but she seems to be muttering about men and their stubbornness.

Jaxcy circled her cabin, seeing the fresh footprints that led from the forest to the cabin and then back to the forest. More than one, she thought. What would have happened if Brennen had not been here? There is nothing here now, she thought. Nothing to hold me here. I know Brennen needs to return to his home, but I am not sure if I am to go with him. He hasn't said. She sighed, her eyes on Kerry as he growled at something he was picking up on. She trusted him in a way that she didn't trust humans.

Hanging her jacket up on the hook near the back door and sliding out of her boots, Jaxcy slowed turned, to find Brennen standing near her, a mug of tea held out for her. He's made himself to home, hasn't he, Lord? But what do I do when he leaves? Even in such a short time, I've gotten used to him being around. I will miss him. With a quiet thank you, she took the mug and then headed for her usual spot on the couch, stopping as his hand rested on her arm.

Brennen looked past her, biting at his lip. He had tried to bring up his phone, but it needed recharging. He knew his friends would be concerned, having been unable to reach him.

"Jaxcy? We need to talk."

She nodded, not looking at him. "I'll make sure you get into town. My truck will run that far, I think. It's really not that far. You can catch the ferry to Labrador and then a plane from there. Your friends must be concerned." She waited for him to remove his hand, frowning when he didn't. She looked up at him, wondering at how tall he was. Jaxcy had always been teased about how short she was, and that had affected how she saw herself. She didn't understand or know that Brennen saw not a short woman, but a beautiful petite lady who could take care of herself. "Brennen?"

"We do need to talk, Jaxcy." He sighed before he swung an arm around her and walked her over to the couch, waiting until she was seated before he dropped down beside her, a prayer raising from his heart for wisdom.

"Brennen? What is it?" Jaxcy's eyes closed. "I know what it is. You are planning on leaving. I'll take you into town. There is a ferry that leaves tonight that you can catch." When he didn't respond, she looked up at him, to find him studying her.

"I'm not leaving, Jaxcy, not without you. I repeat, I will not leave you here. With us marrying before you turned twenty-eight, that has changed everything for you. Now that you have thwarted his plans, he will be after you for revenge."

"But, what about you? Aren't you in danger?" Her voice was barely audible.

"He will be after me, I suppose. That's why we'll head back to Ontario as soon as we can." He saw the moment she caught his words and stared at him, her mouth open. "I am not leaving you here. For one thing, I need to protect you. You need someone to do that for you. Most important? You are my wife, my bride. It doesn't matter how it happened. You are my family. I protect my family and take care of them." He suddenly grinned. "I need to introduce you to eight other ladies."

"Eight ladies? Why? I don't understand."

Brennen began to laugh. "Eight of my friends have gone through what we term as adventures. They have each married a wonderful lady. Some to save each other's life. I'll let them tell you their stories, but one thing is clear. God protected them and brought them through what they faced."

"They did? Eight of them? How many of you are there?"

He laughed harder. "There are twelve of us, all orphans. Then, there is Breck, and then Barnabas."

Jaxcy continued to stare at him. "You're serious!"

"I am." He reached for her hands, bowing his head to pray, asking for guidance for them and protection for Jaxcy. She wondered that he didn't ask that for himself.

Brennen reached for his mug of tea, sipping slowly, giving himself time to compose himself and to find the words he needed to say.

"Brennen?" Jaxcy's hand rested lightly on his until he flipped his over and clasped hers.

"Jaxcy? I need to head for home. I can't leave you here on your own. Please? Come with me? I pledge to do my best to protect you, to give you all the honour that you deserve." He waited, his eyes on hers, as she searched him and then her own heart. He saw the moment that she made her decision, and he drew a deep breath, ready to contact Barnabas and tell him he wasn't coming back.

"I will, Brennen. God help me, I will. I have nothing here. I can barely put food on my table. I scrape and scratch for what I have." She waved her hand to indicate the cabin. "This is all I have. I lost everything in town when Mom and Dad were killed in a landslide. This is all I could find. It has been so hard." She didn't cry, she had done enough of that.

"Thank you, Jaxcy. Now, what do you need to pack to take with you? Did you say there was a ferry tonight?"

"There should be, provided they can run it. We need to leave soon, though." She was on her feet, heading for the bedroom.

"Jaxcy, wait. What do you need to pack out here?"

She spun. "Just the stuff in the desk. The rest doesn't matter. I need Kerry's crate, his food, or enough to get by with, his harness, leash, and his grooming tools. Oh, and his toys." She spun back and almost ran for the bedroom. She felt relieved, able to escape the life she had been living, just existing, she thought.

Finally, standing on the ferry deck, watching the land fade into the distance, she drew a deep breath. This is is, Lord, isn't it? My past is there. My present is here, with a man I don't know, that I am married to. My future? That's in Your hands. You know the path I will walk. My hand is in Yours. Lead, please, Lord.

Jaxcy's hand tucked tightly in his, Brennen watched her face closely, not surprised that there was no emotion on it. She seemed to hide her emotions. I need to talk to her about that, Lord, don't I? I need her to talk to me. He pulled her backward with him, to the sheltered alcove that they had claimed as their own, Kerry in his crate, the bag with his belongings resting on top of his crate, the one bag that Jaxcy had packed sitting beside it. That saddened him, and he became determined to change that.

*Chapter 3*

It was late when they disembarked the ferry, Brennen carrying Kerry's crate and one of the bags, Jaxcy carrying the other one, her free hand tight in his. She was shaking slightly, her emotions suddenly mixed and overwhelming her. She refused to say anything, not realizing that Brennen had picked up on what she was feeling.

Brennen searched for a free area and spying one, headed over there, setting down the crate and bag and just sweeping her into a tight hug. Jaxcy was surprised, her body stiffening before she relaxed against him, hearing his quiet prayer in her ears.

He leaned back finally, his eyes on her face. "Okay?"

"I think so. Just overwhelmed. I have never been on the mainland, in all my life. Is that strange?"

Brennen shrugged. "Not necessarily. If you had no reason to come here, then I guess you wouldn't have." He looked around. "We need to find a ride to the airport. I'm not sure what time the planes leave."

"Brennen!"

Hearing his name called, Brennen jumped and spun, shoving Jaxcy behind him, a frown on his face that smoothed out.

"Andy? Brody? You two are here?" He reached to shake the pilot's hand and then reached to shake Brody's.

"Barnabas sent us. He hadn't heard from you as you had arranged. When he couldn't raise you, he sent us. We just flew in today and were heading for the ferry to go over but found out we had missed it. We were putting in time when we saw you." Brody's face turned to a frown as he heard a dog woofing. "Brennen? Where's the dog?"

"Right here. He's named Kerry, and he's coming with me." Brennen turned slightly, watching Jaxcy as she hid behind him, slight fear showing on her face. "It's okay, Jaxcy. These are friends. And our transportation home."

Brody tilted his head, watching the black-haired beauty trying her best to hide behind Brennen. He frowned. "Brennen? Care to introduce us?"

"Brody, Andy. This is Jaxcy. She's been a friend in need. But I need to give her full name." Brennen watched as she shook her head. "We have to, Jaxcy. We have to. These are friends. They will help us. Andy is the Foundation pilot. We don't have to search for a flight and then wait for it to leave."

"Brennen?" Jaxcy's voice was quiet.

"It is okay." Without taking his eyes from her, or dropping her hand, he spoke. "Brody. Andy. This is Jaxcy Joelyn Dering Connolly. She is my bride, my princess. We are off on an adventure, just like the others."

Andy stared at him. "Who beat you up, Brennen? The bruises haven't faded yet."

"No, they haven't. It's kind of a long story, but I was beaten when I arrived in Jaxcy's town. She stepped in, married me, and then took care of me."

"Welcome to the family, Jaxcy." Brody stepped to the side where he could see her better, seeing the fear in her face. "How be we move off then? Andy has a car here that we rented. Let's head for it."

Brennen nodded, watching as Andy and Brody gathered up their bags, and moved away before he followed, Jaxcy's hand in his.

"Brennen?"

"It's okay, Princess. It's okay. Andy will fly us back to Ontario, to our home. You will be welcomed and loved, just for you. And you will be welcomed and loved because you are my family."

"But they don't know me! How could he say that?"

"Brody? He said it because he means it. He's not one of the ones who have married. But I can tell you that Baird and Berneen married something similar to us. She married him to save his life. One of our friends is our pastor. He was there and forced to marry them. Blair married Cadee to bring her to safety from a war-torn country." He opened the car door, waiting for her to slide in before he shared a long look with Brody, who nodded.

Brody slide into the front passenger's seat, his eyes on the mirror on the door as he closed it, a frown on his face. Brennen was being followed. Who knows what would have happened if he and Andy had not shown up? He was interested to hear Brennen's story but knew Brennen would wait until they could all meet. He shifted slightly to watch the couple in the back seat.

Brennen kept Jaxcy's hand tight in his, shifting his gaze to where the dog crate sat on the seat beside her. He could hear low whines coming from Kerry and knew that Andy would insist on the dog being let out of the crate once they were in the air. Bradon had often traveled with Andy, taking his Australian Shepherd, Kade, with him. Kade was always allowed to roam the cabin unless there was bad weather or turbulence or when they were taking off or landing.

"You'll be able to rest once we're in the air, Princess." Brennen's hand tightened on hers. "I know Andy will have stocked the plane with food." He looked towards Andy. "Do you have coffee, Andy?"

"Gee, that's the one thing I forgot to pack, Brennen." Andy grinned as Brennen shook a finger at him. "Devaney made sure that I had a large supply. For some reason, she thought you would need it."

"Bless her. I do. Nothing against the broth or tea that you supplied, Jaxcy, but I miss my coffee."

"Why? It's so bitter." Jaxcy made a face, causing the men to grin.

# Chapter 4

Seated in one of the seats in the plane, knowing Andy was flying them home through the night, Brennen felt fatigue settling in on him. Jaxcy had dozed off, Kerry tight in her arms, a blanket covering them. He had tucked a pillow under her head, a sleepy thank you his reward. He frowned down at his cup of coffee, suddenly not wanting it. He wanted a mug of tea shared with Jaxcy in her cabin.

"Brennen? Are you okay?" Brody's quiet voice broke the silence in the cabin.

Brennen shrugged. "I don't know. Physically, I know I am healing. Emotions are all over the place, as you can imagine. She's had a rough life, and it's about to get a lot rougher. Jaxcy said her parents were killed in a landslide when she was seventeen and she's been on her own since then. Her home was taken from her, and I am not too sure how legal that was. She was living out in the boonies, no electricity, only wood for heating. She carried in her water to use, heating it if she needed hot water." He glanced at her. "It was a rough place, Brody. One of the worst places I have ever seen."

"I'm glad you're bringing her home, but I don't understand how you ended up married."

"There's a lot to it. One is a law about strangers in their town, either having to marry or end up in jail. Jaxcy pulled out paperwork last night. She had to marry by the time she was twenty-eight to inherit wealth or it went into a trust and the trust turned over to someone we know. Dylan Smithers."

"Smithers? I knew he was slimy but how does he figure into this?"

"That I'm not sure of. More research for us, I guess. She turned twenty-eight a couple of days ago." Brennen sobered even more. "Do you know, she told me that she has never ever celebrated a birthday since her parents died. No one helped her to do that."

"Oh, Brennen. That's sad. We'll make up for that, if she'll let us." He paused, a thought crossing his mind. "Smithers? Isn't he living on that property bordering us?"

"He is. And it happens to belong to Jaxcy. I can see a fight on our hands to get him out of there."

"Dallas will help. Or Will." Brody mentioned a detective friend of theirs and the police chief of the town they lived near.

Brennen yawned, setting down his mug and reaching for a blanket. "Sorry, Brody. I'm still rocky to some extent. The men who met me in her town beat me badly. Jaxcy and her minister stepped in." Brennen's voice died away as he slept.

Brody watched him for a while before his attention turned to Jaxcy, and then to Kerry, finding the dog watching him with bright eyes.

Rousing as the plane landed on the Foundation airstrip, Brennen rubbed at his eyes before he shook out his blanket and folded it. He rose, stretched, and then helped Brody tidy up the cabin. He stood, his eyes on Jaxcy, who still slept, Kerry in her arms. Reaching for the dog and tucking him into his crate, Brennen undid Jaxcy's seatbelt and then gathered her close, surprised at how little she weighed before he nodded to Brody and followed the other man down the steps. Brody tucked the dog's crate onto a seat and then walked back towards Andy, who was approaching him.

"Did he say much, Brody?" Andy was concerned.

"Not a whole lot. We need to watch for Smithers. He's involved." Brody shook his head.

"I just don't get it. How did Brennen get involved?"

"That I don't know. He hasn't said. Nor has Barnabas. We didn't have a lot of time to get any information, other than we needed to leave right away, that he hadn't heard from Brennen." Brody stood for a moment, his eyes on Brennen, who had wrapped an arm around Jaxcy and laid his head down on hers. "He's in love."

Andy ducked his head to study the couple. "He is. He's like the others. Love at first sight. I would not have thought that nine of our friends would have fallen in love so quickly. Let's get them home."

Jaxcy roused as Brennen shut the apartment door behind them, a quiet word of thanks to Brody and Andy. She stared around and then pushed at him, dropping to her feet, a hand rubbing at her eyes.

"Where are we?" She was confused.

"In my, sorry, our apartment in the Foundation building. That's something that we didn't talk about. Each of us has our own apartment here. And an office on the main floor." He watched her closely before he reached to switch on more lights. "Head off to bed, Princess. There are three bedrooms. Take your pick."

Jaxcy nodded, not quite awake enough to understand totally what he was saying. With a soft thank you, she reached for her bag, noting that someone had let Kerry out of his crate. Brennen watched her walk down the hall, pausing at each doorway to study the room, before he turned to reach for Kerry's leash, closing the door softly behind him as he walked the dog outside.

Brennen yawned as he hung up his jacket and then the leash, fatigue hitting him. He squinted at his watch. Three in the morning, he thought. Not a lot of time to sleep, but he would catch what he could. He strode towards his bedroom, changed, and then slid under the covers, startled for a moment before he smiled. He simply reached to cradle Jaxcy near to him. He felt Kerry jump on the bed and then curl up tight to his legs. This is what I have been missing, isn't it, Lord? A family. He slept even as his prayer of thanks rose.

—

# Chapter 5

Early the next morning, Jaxcy rose, staring back at Brennen before she moved to claim her clothes and then search the apartment. She stood in awe of the bathrooms in each bedroom before choosing one, her hands on the soft, thick, aqua-coloured towels that filled the towel racks. Tears blinded her for a moment. She had never had or seen such luxury in her life.

Heading for the kitchen finally, she stopped to study each room, thinking that her cabin would have fit at least three times in the apartment. She paled at the thought of having to clean it but then stiffened her spine and decided that as Brennen's wife, that was exactly what she would do. She didn't have training in anything else.

Surprise halted her forward walk as she stood in the kitchen doorway. Jaxcy walked around, her hand touching the appliances and then the smaller appliances on the counter. Opening a door, she stood once more, her mouth open as she stared at the well-stocked pantry. She shook her head, finding reaching for a loaf of bread.

Brennen stood, in turn, watching her, Kerry tight to his leg. Sadness filled his heart for a moment, knowing what she had come from. He could not imagine living as she had.

"Jaxcy?" Brennen's voice startled her. "I see you have the loaf of bread. You don't have to have toast, you know?"

"I don't? It's what I usually have." She hesitated, then set the loaf of bread back down, unsure of herself.

"You can if you wish. I didn't mean you couldn't." Brennen stepped towards her, an arm around her shoulders. "We have cereal if you like cereal. Hot or cold. There are waffles in the freezer. There is probably fresh fruit in the fridge as well as eggs."

"All that? I don't know, Brennen. This is so hard." Tears sparkled in her eyes, turning them almost black.

Brennen sighed, reaching to hug her. "It's okay, Jaxcy. I'm sorry. I didn't mean to lay it out so roughly for you. I'm not sure how to treat a lady in my life."

"I'm no lady." Jaxcy pushed at him.

Brennen refused to let her go. "You are, Jaxcy. You are a very beautiful lady. One that I am so glad to have in my life. You are a princess, and don't let anyone tell you any different." He felt her finally relax.

"So, what do we have to eat?" She refused to answer the unspoken question in his voice.

"What would you like? Tell me and I'll cook for you." When she refused to tell him, he simply moved her to the kitchen, seated her, and then prepared their breakfast.

Jaxcy rose to clear away the dishes, awe on her face when he pulled open the dishwasher.

"A dishwasher? I've never seen one." She watched as he stacked their dishes and then turned to her.

"Jaxcy, we need to talk, but I'm not sure if this is the right time or not. Come. Let's head for the office. I have some paperwork in there that I need to do, but I want to start us off with prayer."

She nodded, reaching down to scoop Kerry into her arms. "Kerry? Has he been out?"

"He has. He's already made some friends."

Jaxcy frowned. "That is unusual. Where do I walk him?"

"I'll show you." Brennen reached to retrieve a set of keys from his desk. "Here. These are yours. I'll show you which keys work which doors."

Brennen finally sat back, his hand still holding hers, a frown on his face. "We'll need to meet with Barnabas. But I really don't know what to do."

"I'm not sure what you mean." Jaxcy watched him closely.

"I mean. We need to start investigating Smithers and your property. We need to get some advice on what your trust is." He sighed. "They told me not to have an adventure. We told Brendon it ended with him. It doesn't look as if it did."

"Brennen? What are you talking about? Who is Brendon? What adventures?" Jaxcy was confused.

Brennen began to laugh. "Eight of my friends here at the Foundation had what we call adventures, some life-threatening. But through it all, they met the loves of their lives. In fact, Brandon and Hagen are new parents to a set of twins. There are eight ladies who will welcome you. If you feel overwhelmed, tell them or tell me. They don't mean to do that, but they can."

"I see. It's been so many years since I've had a friend. Even then, they were not close friends." She sighed, her head going down against his arm.

"Speak up for yourself." He sighed as he heard a knock at the door. "We're not finished our talk yet, Princess. Let me see who is there. Look around here. I want your input on what we should change. This is your home. We need to make it that for you." Having said that, he rose and walked away, leaving her staring after him, her arms tightening around Kerry.

"Did he mean that, Kerry? Did he really mean that? I feel as if I died and went to heaven. That God heard my grumbling and shoved me into something so wonderful, just to shut me up." Tears sparkled on her cheeks before she swiped angrily at them.

Barnabas Carey stood beside Brennen, his eyes on Jaxcy, hearing her words, and hearing Brennen's faint muttering. He had stopped by, Brody letting them know that they were home and that he really needed to talk to Brennen. Brody had not told him what was up, but his very silence had alerted Barnabas.

Brennen simply sat beside her, swept her into a hug, and prayed for her. She was startled at his quick movements but then listened to his interceding on her behalf. She wondered at that, not used to it.

—

Jaxcy realized suddenly that they were not alone, as her startled eyes saw Barnabas sitting quietly near them, his head bowed as Brennen prayed before he took up the petition.

# Chapter 6

Smiling at Jaxcy, Barnabas waited for Brennen to speak, knowing his friend was having difficulty forming his words. He finally shook his head.

"I'm Barnabas Carey." He frowned for a moment as Kerry alerted and then jumped from Jaxcy's lap to head towards him, standing up to sniff at his face. "Does your dog always do that?" He was grinning as he held out a hand for Kerry to sniff at.

"He does. He has never bitten anyone yet. That's Kerry. He's protective of me."

"I would imagine he would be. Now, tell me about yourself. Brennen seems tongue-tied at the moment."

Brennen began to laugh. "And that is unusual for me, is what you're not saying. This is Jaxcy Joelyn Derring Connolly." At Barnabas' quick look at him, he nodded. "We are married. There is a story there. You can see by the bruising that I was attacked when I arrived. Jaxcy stepped in. There is a law in her town that if a stranger stops in and doesn't marry someone from the town, then they are jailed. I don't remember it at all, but Jaxcy tells me she felt she had to." He tilted his head to watch her face. "This is the J.J. Dering I was to meet."

"She is? We didn't know, did we? Thank you, Jaxcy. Welcome to the family."

Jaxcy finally remembered to snap her mouth closed. "Thank you. That wasn't what I expected."

"It wasn't?" Barnabas nodded. "I know what you expected. You expected blame and recriminations, to be made to feel like an outsider, not wanted?" At her nod and sad look, he shared a look with Brennen. "That doesn't happen here, Jaxcy. All of the eight men who are married faced danger, but we all stood by one another. It made us closer. The eight ladies of the Foundation building are close. I am sure they will welcome you into their midst. Anna, Doc's wife, will be around, I suspect, once she hears about you. Now, talk to me." He glanced at his watch. "We are in no rush. Take your time. We will meet later with the men, Brennen. This afternoon, late afternoon, after they're all home."

Jaxcy sighed. "I don't know where to begin. My parents were killed in a landslide when I was sixteen or seventeen. It was right around my birthday. I lost the house. The bank just took it. They shouldn't have. Dad had insurance that would have paid it off and let me live in it. The only place I could find was a little cabin in the woods and I found a truck to use." She looked up at Brennen, resignation in her glance. "I didn't have a lot, scratching and scraping to survive."

"Her house was a little cabin, Barnabas. She had only a fireplace and wood stove for heating and cooking. No electricity. No running water." He hugged her to him, even as he looked up at Barnabas. "This is such a contrast for her."

"I am sure it is. You mentioned Smithers?"

"I did. The land and house he is using? It belongs to Jaxcy. We need to talk to someone about evicting him. She also had stocks and bonds that we will need the accountant to look at and explain to her. I took a quick glance, but I'm not into numbers."

"We can do that. Now, Jaxcy? May I call you that?" At her nod, Barnabas paused for a moment, his eyes on the floor before he looked up at her. "What can we do for you? I can only imagine that Brennen wants to do what he can for you. So do we."

Jaxcy shrugged, unable to say what she needed to. She didn't want to be obliged to the Foundation, not fully realizing that she was now part of a family.

"I need to take her shopping, Barnabas." Brennen simply shared a look with Barnabas, who nodded. "Today, I think."

Jaxcy looked at him, horrified, before he simply shook his head.

"We will, Jaxcy. Trust me. Please?" He waited until she nodded. "Anything else, Barnabas?"

The other man shrugged. "I'm not sure, Brennen. Let me have what you can of the documents. I'll talk to Dallas and Will and see what we can do about the property. I would suggest that Jaxcy not go near there until I have."

"No, it's not likely a good idea." Brennen was silent, just nodding when Barnabas stood and said his good-byes.

Jaxcy finally shifted away from Brennen, her arms wrapping around herself.

"Jaxcy? If you don't want to go shopping, I'm fine with that."

"No, it's not that." She blinked rapidly, finding tears almost overcoming her once more. "It's that I don't have any money, Brennen."

"Jaxcy? Please look at me." Brennen waited until she did. "You are my bride. It is part of my duty and honour to provide for you." He sighed. "There is something else. When we marry, the Foundation provides for our wives. They are paid wages, just like we are. It's part of the Foundation premise of encouraging."

"They can't. Not for me. They don't know me." Jaxcy would have continued to protest but Brennen's finger was laid on her lips.

"No, they don't. It doesn't matter. This is what they do."

"I've never heard of that before." She watched as Brennen rose to his feet, heading for his desk, to pull open a drawer and remove something.

Brennen stared down at the small ring box that he held in his hands. It was the only thing that he had left of his parents, his mother's engagement ring. He couldn't remember them, but he felt certain that they would approve of his bride. He simply returned to sit beside her, reached for her hand, and slipped on the ruby ring, her mouth opening and closing before she looked up at him. He nodded and then reached to hug her.

# Chapter 7

Feeling eyes on him, Brennen shifted his stance as he waited in the clothing store for Jaxcy. She was feeling overwhelmed, he knew, but when one of the ladies from the building had approached him, he had quickly introduced her to Fynn, his friend, Brady's wife, who simply took Jaxcy under her wing and led her away. He could hear Fynn's quick laughter and comments, but not a lot of talking from Jaxcy. That concerned him.

His eyes searched the store before he moved to look out the window, his eyes finding the short thin man standing across the road, his focus on the building. Smithers! How did he know? Brennen reached for his phone, sending off a quick text to Barnabas.

Jaxcy approached him, Fynn beside her, bags in their hands.

"I spent too much, Brennen. I just know I did." Jaxcy had a tight, worried look on her face. It was obvious she was not used to spending money without counting every penny.

Fynn hugged her, surprising her. "No, you didn't. Brennen would say that. Besides, I had fun helping you. If you want to shop at any time, come find me. I'll gladly come with you. So would any of the others. See you two later." She was away before Jaxcy could respond.

"She's like that, Jaxcy."

"She is? She's so down to earth. I like her." She took the hand that Brennen was holding out.

"She is. Would you believe she is a doctor?" He laughed at the look Jaxcy gave him. "She is. Fynn is an entomologist. I'll take you out to her building one day." He stuffed the packages into his truck and then pointed across the road. "Come, let's go out for lunch. We need to celebrate."

"Brennen! I have cost you so much already."

"No, you haven't. I want to." He held the door for her, his eyes on Smithers, seeing the instance the man recognized Jaxcy. He sighed to himself. Now what, Lord? How do I protect her?

Their lunch finished, Brennen reached for Jaxcy's hand as they exited the small, family-style restaurant. He had had to persuade her to have what she wanted, not just what was the simplest or the cheapest. She had frowned at him, and he had thought she looked just adorable when she did so.

"Now what, Brennen? I should get back to Kerry. He's not used to me being away from him for long." Jaxcy was worried about her companion.

"We'll go get him and take him for a long walk. How's that? I can show you some of the gardens, even though they are not in bloom yet."

"Okay. Do you have time?"

"For you, I will always have time. You will come first with me, right after God. I want you to understand that." Brennen waited until she looked back up at him and then nodded.

Jaxcy opened her mouth to respond when a look of horror crossed her face. Before she could even scream, Brennen's hand was torn away from her as he was tackled and taken down to the pavement. She stood for a moment, watching as Brennen was struck repeatedly before she ran forward, throwing herself at the man's back, her hands scrabbling and scratching at his face.

The man simply shook Jaxcy off, swinging her around to face him by the arm that he held in a tight grip, before his fist struck her violently in the face, not once but twice, sending her to the pavement, to tumble over and over and then to lay sprawled facedown, not moving. The man stood for a moment watching her, hearing the sounds of shouts and running feet coming his way. He turned back to Brennen, a booted foot coming back before he kicked the younger man in the ribs with the steel toe of that boot. He shot a look over his shoulder and then scuttled away down the nearby alley, like the cowardly bully he was.

Smithers knew how to hit and run. He had been doing that all his life. He ran for the car that was waiting, scrambling in before it tore away. The two men who had chased him were too late. They could only stand and stare at the dust raised, obscuring the car, before they shook their heads and ran back towards the street.

Brody and Branigan ran forward, ready to help. They could hear the rise and fall of sirens in the distance, drawing near.

"It's Brennen!" Branigan was on his knees, his hands trying to keep Brennen from moving.

"Let me up! I need to find Jaxcy!" Brennen fell back, his head spinning, a hand cradling his ribs. He shook off the hands, trying to rise.

Brady, another friend, and a paramedic, slowed his steps. "Brennen?" He shared a look with his partner, Patrick, even as they stopped their forward movement with the stretchers.

"Yeah." Branigan looked around, not seeing Brody for the people crowded around them. "Where's Brody?"

"He's here?" Brady looked at the officers who had responded. "We need these people moved back. We can't work like this."

The officers nodded, before with arms outstretched, they moved the men and women back and began to take statements.

"Brody?" Brady shot him a glance even as he tried to restrain Brennen.

Brennen kept shoving at the hands preventing him from reaching Jaxcy. He needed to know she was alive and okay. It didn't matter about him, he thought.

"Jaxcy?" He slumped back to the pavement, his hand coming up to wipe at the blood that had started to trickle from his mouth. "Where is she?"

"Jackie? Who's that?" Brady reached to try and take Brennen's vitals, his partner with Jaxcy.

"Jaxcy." Brennen shoved harder against Brady. "Brady, move. I need to get up."

"No, you need to stay still. You're hurt, Brennen. I need to find out where."

Brennen rose to his hands and knees and crawled away from Brady, despite Brady's best efforts and protests to keep him where he was. He collapsed beside Jaxcy, a hand out to touch the back of her head, a groan coming from him as he lost his fight to stay alert.

# Chapter 8

Brody's hands were there to help as Patrick worked on Jaxcy, his eyes shifting to watch Brady as best he can.

"Who is she, Brody?" Branigan stood behind him, worry on his face.

"Jaxcy? She's Brennen's wife." His concentration on Jaxcy, he didn't see the looks the other three men exchanged.

"His wife? What are you talking about?" Brady turned as an officer approached to help shift Brennen to a stretcher.

"A long story, Brady. One that we were to hear this afternoon at our meeting." Brody stood, his eyes on Jaxcy.

"How is Jackie, Patrick?" Brady shot a glance at her as she was transferred carefully to another stretcher.

"It's not Jackie, Brady. It's Jaxcy." Brody spelled it out for him. "What now, fellows?"

"Off to Emerge. One of too many trips we've made today." Patrick rose, his hand on Jaxcy's wrist as the stretcher she had been placed on was raised.

"Brody, you're riding with them?" Branigan had his phone out, ready to make the call that they always dreaded making.

"I am. Jaxcy knows me, to some degree. I met her last night when Andy and I tracked them down in Labrador."

Branigan nodded, his attention on the call he had placed.

"Barnabas? Brennen and Jaxcy have been assaulted. How bad? I'm not sure, but it looks bad. No one can tell us who or why. What's that? Smithers? Him? Who knows. Brody is riding with Brady and Patrick. What's that?" Branigan covered one ear to hear Barnabas better over the chatter around him, moving away from the scene and towards his truck. "No. Brennen was conscious, sort of, when we arrived. Jaxcy, is it? It is? She was unconscious. Sure. I'll keep you updated as I can. You're heading in? Oh, after that conference call? Okay. If anything changes, I'll call." Branigan's phone was tossed on the passenger's seat as he pulled away, knowing that it could well mean life and death for his friend. He shook his head. He had not expected to hear that Brennen had married. That was a story that he really wanted to hear.

Doc looked around as Brady and Patrick wheeled the stretchers in, the nurses helping.

"Brady? Who do you have?"

"Brennen. He's not great, Doc. It looks as if he took a bad blow to his ribs. He's bleeding from the lung, I am assuming." He nodded to the other stretcher. "That's Jaxcy. She's taken a bad blow or two to her face."

Patrick spoke up. "When I touched it, she whimpered and moved away from my hand. I couldn't get a good feel of how bad it is."

Doc nodded, before pointing towards the rooms. "In there. Brennen? Can you hear me?"

Brennen's eyes flickered before his lips formed Jaxcy's name. "Jaxcy? Where is she?"

"Jaxcy's here, Brennen. I need to examine you." Doc's hand on Brennen's chest kept him still. "Brennen, you need to stay still."

Brennen moved to roll to his side, let out a groan, and then laid still, his face whitening from the pain.

Later, Doc stood beside Jaxcy's bedside, his eyes on the computer monitor showing the X-Rays she had had taken. He shook his head. Not a total fracture, he thought. Hairline at best. She would be sore.

He turned as he heard footsteps, and Barnabas walked towards him.

"Barnabas? You're here?"

"I am. First, Brennen?"

"Pneumothorax. A punctured lung from a rib. He took a heavy blow. There is also a lot of old bruising." Doc sent him a questioning look.

"Yeah, about that. He was beaten badly about a week ago. He told me this morning he had been in the hospital there for a day or so, and then moved to a home. He thought he was recovering."

"He had been, but this beating sets him back. He'll be in for a few days. The surgeon on call is heading in. We'll need to place a chest tube."

"Ouch." Barnabas studied his friend's wife. "I'll sign off on his paperwork. Jaxcy is not able to."

"What on earth are you talking about?" Doc spun, a questioning look on his face.

"Jaxcy? She and Brennen are married. A long story, Doc, but apparently she saved him from going to jail in her hometown. How is she?"

Doc shook his head, and Barnabas grinned at his muttering about the younger generation and how they met their ladies. He nodded at Jaxcy.

"There is a hairline fracture of her jaw. The surgeon will take a look at her as well. Likely she'll need it wired for a few weeks to heal. Find who did this."

"We're working on it, Doc." Barnabas watched Jaxcy for a few minutes, his heart rising in prayer for the young woman before he turned, walking across the hall to stand beside Brennen before he moved to the waiting room, his eyes searching the faces gathered there, a faint smile on his face. It was as he had expected. The Foundation building fellows were there as were the ladies. He could see Anna, Doc's wife, as well.

Brody approached him, his eyes looking past him.

"How are they?"

Barnabas shook his head. "Both are heading for surgery. Brennen has a punctured lung and needs a chest tube. Jaxcy has a hairline fracture of her jaw." Barnabas frowned. "She is so tiny."

"I know. Brennen didn't say too much, but I got the impression that she didn't have a lot. He said she lived in a really ramshackle cabin, no electricity, no running water, with little income."

Buckley, the minister in the group, spoke from beside him. "Who is Jaxcy, is it?"

Barnabas sighed, his eyes sliding closed even as he prayed for his friend and his bride. "Buckley, we need to meet as a group. See if we can use a room here. That will free up the waiting room for others."

"We can. I already asked." Buckley moved away, a puzzled look turned back towards his friends, before he started moving among their group, to shuffle them from the waiting room to a conference room nearby.

# Chapter 9

Looking around the room from where he stood speaking with Will Peters, the police chief of the town, and Dallas, a detective who was also a good friend, Barnabas studied each one who was present. He didn't have a lot of information to give them and that concerned him. Brennen had handed him the package of documents on his way out of the building with Jaxcy but he had not had a chance to more than glance through them.

"You suspect Smithers?" Dallas had had his own problems with Smithers in the past.

"We do. Brennen didn't get a chance to go into too many details but Jaxcy owns the property he has been using. She had forgotten, I guess. There is also a trust fund that came to her when she married Brennen and then had her birthday. Brennen suspects Smithers was after that."

"I'm sure he was." Will gave a sound of frustration as his phone vibrated. He squinted at the number. "I need to take this. I'll be back."

"Barnabas, what do you really know about her?" Dallas asked.

"Not a lot. Brennen had a letter before he went east, asking that he contact a J.J. Dering. Breck, he and I talked about it, prayed it over, and he decided to go. We didn't know that Jaxcy was that person."

Dallas shook his head. "And he ended up married to her? There's a story there."

"There is. I need to tell the others. I have some documents that we'll need to take a look at. Brennen handed them over to me." Barnabas moved away, heading for Buckley who nodded.

Barnabas stood for a moment, studying each one who was in the room before he nodded. He knew the hearts of the men and the ladies and that they would do their utmost to help Brennen. He had always been there for them.

"Okay, fellows, ladies. This is what is up. As you know, just over a week ago, Brennen headed for the east coast, to meet someone named J.J. Dering. When he arrived in that town, he was badly beaten. A young woman stepped in to help him, along with the minister of her church. There is a law in that town that states that any stranger who arrives must marry someone from that town or go to jail." He paused, hearing the low murmurs and then the nods. "Brennen was married that same day. Unknown to him at the time, the J. J. Dering he was to meet was a young woman. Her full name is Jaxcy Joelyn Dering. She is the one who stepped in and married our friend, to save him from jail. From what research I have been able to do, it is a long sentence that they are given."

Benen spoke up. "Is that the lady who was with him today?"

"It is, Benen. Andy and Brody flew down yesterday at my request, as Brennen did not check in with me as we had arranged. They found Brennen and

Jaxcy heading for an airport, returning this way." He looked around. "Bradon? She has a dog that I would ask you to take care of for now."

"How are they, Barnabas?" Burnie spoke up, worry on his face, and in his voice.

"Brennen has a punctured lung from the beating today. Doc says it looks as if he was brutally kicked. Jaxcy was also assaulted and has a fractured jaw." He tamped down the anger rising in him. "This is now how we welcome people to our town."

"Do we know who?" This from Brandon, Hagen's arm around her husband.

"We do. Dylan Smithers." Dallas looked up from his notes. "From what Barnabas has learned from Brennen, Jaxcy is the owner of the property he has been living on. She was unaware of that until a few days ago. Barnabas, you have paperwork to turn over to me?"

"I do." He handed over the envelope he had been worrying with his hands. "I took a quick look. Deeds and other papers."

Dallas nodded. "Good. We need to stop Smithers. He's been the bane of everyone's existence for years. We just had not been able to prove anything."

"We can from today. There are numerous witnesses to the assault." Will Peters spoke from where he was leaning against the wall.

"That's good." Barnabas stared down at the floor, letting his friends talk among themselves. He looked around as the door opened and Doc looked in, beckoning at him to come out.

"Doc?" Barnabas spoke as soon as the door closed behind him.

"Brennen is headed for surgery now. I just wanted you to know. The surgeon felt he couldn't wait any longer."

Barnabas drew a deep breath. "We've been through so much with all of the fellows. God has provided and healed."

"He has." Doc was silent, his thoughts on his young friends. "Now, Jaxcy? What has that girl been doing to herself? She is underweight."

"I know. She's been on her own since she was seventeen. Brennen said she lived out in the woods in a ramshackle cabin, with no electricity. She scraped for everything she could get."

"We need to fix that, Barnabas. See to it." Doc paced away and then back. "She'll have her jaw wired for a few weeks. This is not going to help her get to where she needs to be."

"I know that, Doc. I know that. I stopped by this morning to talk with Brennen. She will not ask for anything. He mentioned that when he told her there was a lot of food, she put the loaf of bread back, thinking he didn't want her to have toast."

Doc blinked rapidly, his emotions getting the better of him for a moment. "We need to change that. I don't think we've faced that with the others, now have we?" With that, he walked away, leaving

Barnabas to stare at the wall in front of him, his thoughts muddled, unlike him.

# Chapter 10

Fynn slowly approached Jaxcy's bedside, not quite sure of how she would be received. She studied her new friend, wincing at the bruising that was starting to colour her face. Lord, why? This shouldn't have happened. Please, Lord? Heal my friend. Heal Brennen.

Walking away after a time, Fynn sought for Brady, finding him standing right outside the door waiting for her. He simply enveloped her into a hug and stood, his head on hers, his eyes on Jaxcy.

"Was she awake?"

"No, she wasn't. Brady? This had to hurt. Why?"

"Likely to keep her from coming here to get her property. Smithers was to get it if she hadn't married by the time that she was twenty-eight."

"And is she?" Fynn leaned back to look up at him.

"She is. Barnabas said about three days ago." Brady sighed. "We need to do something to help her celebrate. She hasn't celebrated a birthday since her parents died, from what Brennen told Barnabas."

"That's so sad. Was it only this morning that I took her through May's clothing store? She didn't want to spend any money. I had to convince her that was what Brennen wanted."

"It's understandable." Brady looked around. "I have to head back out. You're staying?"

"I am. I have the time. Ennis and Cadee are here as well."

It was after midnight when Jaxcy finally aroused and stayed awake, her eyes opening as she stared around, fear in her heart. She had no idea what had happened until she moved and pain shot through her face. Tears blinded her as she reached to touch the jaw, finding the sore spot. She remembered, then, a man tackling Brennen before she had run at him. Brennen? She sat up abruptly, waiting until her head cleared.

She slipped from the bed, searching for clothes, finding some of the ones that Fynn had convinced her to buy, was it only yesterday? She dressed rapidly and then headed for the open door, stopping for a moment to catch her breath and her balance. Where is Brennen? Lord? Where is he?

Jaxcy looked around for a nurse and didn't see one before she walked quietly down the hallway, searching through the open doors, finally spotting Brennen. Looking over her shoulder, she hesitated before she headed towards him, her hands coming out to grip the bed rail, her eyes on him.

"Brennen, what did I do?" Her voice was barely audible, pain evident on her face. "Why? Why didn't you just stay away?"

Jaxcy stood for hours that way, refusing to move when the nurses suggested that she would be more comfortable in a chair. She simply shook her head. She felt responsible for his being there and just wanted it to be different. Her heart was raised constantly in prayer.

Barnabas stood for a moment in the doorway, watching her, before he moved towards her. He frowned. She had not even noticed that someone else was in the room, her focus solely on Brennen.

"Jaxcy?" His hand went out to help her keep her balance as she jumped. "Should you be here?"

"I have to." He had to strain to hear her words. "I have to. It's my fault."

"No, it's not. It's Smithers' fault." He sighed, knowing that she didn't believe him. "Here, you need to sit. The nurse said you've been standing here for hours."

"I can't. I'm sorry. I need to stay here." Jaxcy looked at him, a tortured look in her eyes. "I have to be here."

"We get that, Jaxcy. All we want is for you to sit. You're hurt as well." Barnabas was growing frustrated.

Brennen had roused as he heard the voices, a frown on his face for a moment, before pain shot through his chest as he moved. His hand reached up to touch hers, causing her to jump.

"Jaxcy? You can sit, Princess. I know you're here." Brennen watched through pain-narrowed eyes.

Jaxcy turned her focus to him. "Brennen? You're awake!"

"I am, Princess. How be you sit?"

Jaxcy just shook her head. "I can't, Brennen. I just can't." She turned and ran from the room, leaving Brennen trying to rise and go after her.

"Stay put, Brennen. I'll find her." Barnabas was out of the room, searching for her, finding her standing in the waiting room, staring out of the window into the growing daylight, Fynn's arm around her.

"Barnabas? Is Brennen worse?" Fynn was confused.

"No. He tried to get Jaxcy to sit. She's been standing by his bed for hours, the nurses have said."

"Jaxcy? Why?" Fynn waited, knowing Jaxcy would talk when she was ready.

"I had to, Fynn. I had to." Jaxcy stopped speaking, her body shutting down, her eyes closing as she collapsed. Barnabas was there to catch her, turning with her in his arms and striding back towards Brennen's room, Fynn beside him.

"Barnabas? Aren't you taking her to her own room?"

Barnabas simply shook his head. "They need to be together. If I don't take her back to Brennen, he'll be up and looking for her. And he can't just now."

Brennen had managed to sit, his legs over the edge of the bed, but the pain had stopped him. He sat, his hand wrapped around his ribs, watching the door.

"Barnabas?"

“She collapsed, Brennen. She has a fractured jaw, which none of us have been able to tell you about yet.”

# Chapter 11

Grimacing in pain as he did so, Brennen slid over on the bed, the arm on his uninjured or less injured side out to cradle Jaxcy as Barnabas laid her beside him. He could hear the soft footsteps as the nurse approached. Worried, he looked up at her.

"Katie?" He was thankful it was one of the nurses that they knew from church.

"She stood here for hours, Brennen. She had been here for a while when we found her. I would say likely five or more hours. We just could not get her to leave." Katie reached to check Jaxcy, a frown on her face. "She just wouldn't leave you, Brennen. Her fingers would be white at times, she was holding on that tight. I don't know that she took her eyes off of you the whole time."

Barnabas shook his head. "Even when I approached her, she didn't look around." He shared a look with Brennen.

"She doesn't have anyone, other than me, Barnabas. She hasn't totally learned to trust me. It will come." He looked up, a tortured look in his eyes. "I pray it is soon. I pray also that she learns to trust the rest of us."

Jaxcy gave a soft moan as she turned her face against Brennen, a flicker of pain crossing her face.

Katie was away and back, ready to give a pain injection when Brennen held up his hand.

"Do we know if she has any allergies?"

Katie paused. "Now, that's a good question. I am not sure that we do." She looked down at the syringe and sighed. "I gather that you're refusing to have her given a shot."

"For now. Until Jaxcy can tell us or we can reach out to the minister in her hometown and see if there are any health concerns. He seems to be the only one she had contact with."

Barnabas shook his head as Katie walked away. He frowned, a thought running through his mind.

"You two didn't talk much?"

"Not about medical stuff." Brennen sighed, pain shooting through him as he moved, and he struggled to breathe. "What did he do to me?"

"Kicked you with his steel-toed boot. Your rib punctured your lung. You have a chest tube for now."

Brennen paled. "How do I take care of Jaxcy?"

"That's where we come in. It's your turn to receive, Brennen. You are always giving to us." Barnabas waited for a while, watching as Brennen dozed off, the pain medications taking hold before he walked away.

Breck walked towards him as he headed for his truck, and he paused, waiting for him to catch up with him.

"How are they?"

"Jaxcy was up. They found her standing by Brennen's bed. She refused to leave. He's been awake. Right now, they're together." He stopped, a thought running through his mind. "Where do we stand with Smithers?"

"He's gone underground by the sounds of it." Breck was frustrated. "I still don't get it."

"Get what?"

"How is Smithers involved? Did Jaxcy know him?"

Barnabas stared down at the keys he was rubbing his fingers on. "I don't know. I got the impression that she didn't."

"Then, I don't get it. How does he fit in?" Breck rubbed at his face, a puzzled look on it.

"That's what we're going to have to determine. You're heading in?" At Breck's nod, Barnabas paused, thinking through his day. "Send out a text message. Whoever is around and free, we'll meet later this afternoon."

"How long is Brennen in for?"

Barnabas shrugged. "Depends on how the lung comes along."

Breck looked up a couple of hours later from the book that he was reading, his attention down the hall. He rose, heading that way, finding Dallas heading his way. He shook his head as he noted the teenager Dallas had a grip on.

"Dallas?" Breck paused, waiting for Dallas to speak.

"I found him outside Brennen's room." Dallas held up an evidence bag, with a switchblade knife in it. "He shouldn't be here. It's not visiting hours. Besides, he's not family or friend to either one of them. Not that I know of."

Breck watched the younger man, seeing the fear flickering in his eyes. "He's been with Smithers, Dallas. I've seen them together."

"He has, hasn't he? I was here to talk to Brennen." Dallas sighed. "Now, I'm off downtown. I'll be back. How are they?"

Breck shrugged, not willing to say much in front of the teenager. "About what you would expect."

Dallas shared a look with him and then, nodding, walked away. Breck stared at the door to Brennen's room before walking towards it, to stand in the doorway. The surgeon was there and he could hear quiet conversation between the two men. He turned away to find Bradon and Burnie walking towards him.

"How is he?" Burnie's question was quiet, but Breck could hear the worry in his voice.

"I haven't talked to him yet. He was sleeping when I got here." Breck pointed towards the waiting room. "Any word from the investigation you fellows are running?"

"Not yet. We're having trouble accessing any records from that town. It's locked down tight." Bradon was frustrated.

"We should be able to access something. Do we even know their marriage is legal?" Burnie was puzzled.

"It is. Barnabas has verified that, he said. The Foundation lawyer is working on that. Apparently, this town has been on the radar of various authorities for years. They just could not prove anything. People were too afraid to talk."

"And it will fall to Brennen to do just that." Bradon paced. "How do we know that the trust fund and the documentation giving it to Smithers is legit?"

"The lawyer is working on that. He's pulled in someone else skilled and accomplished in estate and trust laws."

"That's good." Burnie watched the surgeon walk away from Brennen's room. "Can we see him?"

"Likely. Jaxcy is with him. Barnabas said she found him last night and refused to move from his room."

"Guilt?" Bradon took a guess.

"Likely. Say, did you retrieve Kerry?"

"I did. He and Kade are best friends now." Bradon sobered. "Ennis was in tears last night, Breck. She can't imagine how it came to this point for Jaxcy. Or how she had even lived. Fynn was by our place. The ladies are planning on meeting for prayer, and then to see what they can do for Jaxcy."

# Chapter 12

Walking slowly through the apartment, her hand rubbing at her temple trying to ease her headache, Jaxcy searched for something to do that wouldn't disturb Brennen, who was sleeping. She had stood and watched him, knowing that the effort of coming home had drained his stamina. She sighed. What did I do, Lord? I didn't know we were getting into this. I never meant for him to be hurt.

Finally searching for cleaning supplies, Jaxcy was surprised to find them well stocked, but not well used. She frowned. The apartment was clean, sparkling clean in fact. This did not make sense. She turned to her laundry but was unsure how to even work the washer. She had washed her clothes by hand for years, hanging them to dry in front of the stove in the winter, outside in the better weather.

Heading for the door as she heard a knock, she opened it, frowning at the three women standing there.

"I'm sorry?"

"Hi, Jaxcy. I'm Berneen, Baird's wife. This is Cadee, Benen's wife, and Imly, Brendon's wife. We won't stay for long, but we want to pray with you. Will you let us?"

Jaxcy shrugged, stepping back so they could enter. She pointed down the hall.

"Which room? Kitchen or living room?"

"Kitchen." Cadee held up a tray she had been holding. "I have muffins for us, but some delicious purée for you. If you want, that is." She was suddenly hesitant, not sure if she had overstepped her bounds.

"That's fine." Jaxcy was getting more and more frustrated. "I wish..."

"What do you wish?" Berneen moved around the kitchen, fixing coffee for those who wanted it and then tea for Imly and Jaxcy. She had heard Jaxcy liked her tea, not realizing that it had been all Jaxcy could afford.

Jaxcy shook her head, pointing to her jaw. "This. Why?"

"Because you are standing in his way. Brennen as well. He's known to be a mean, vindictive man." Cadee looked up from where she had been fixing the purée for her. "Benen said he's been like for as long as he has known him. The victims are too terrified to speak up."

"So, that leaves me?" The three ladies had to strain to hear Jaxcy's voice.

"I guess. We have all had that, Jaxcy. Had to stand up for ourselves and our fellows. To bring evil to justice." Imly's hand was laid on the one Jaxcy had on the table. "It's not easy. Some of us have almost died. Ennis did. She was stabbed. Bradon was actually drowned and revived. My Brendon was shot trying to protect me and then disappeared for four weeks."

Jaxcy's eyes were on her, wonder in her eyes. "There is no way that happens."

Cadee laughed. "It does. Berneen here? Forced to marry Baird to save his life. Me? Benen married me, as my father's request, to protect me and bring me home from a foreign country. I almost died from a poisoning."

Jaxcy studied each woman. "Where was God?"

"Right there. Even at the darkest point, He was there. He did not walk away from any one of us." Berneen sat beside Jaxcy, an arm around her. "He is here with you, Jaxcy, with Brennen. If Brennen had not married you, you would not have survived. Smithers would have seen to that."

Cadee began to pray, with the other two ladies following suit. Jaxcy was quiet, not saying much because of her injury, but she also was not sure how to talk with other ladies. She had never been comfortable doing that.

Jaxcy jumped as she felt an arm come around her and a kiss was dropped on her temple. Brennen slipped into the seat beside her, a word of thanks for the cup of coffee Cadee slid in front of him.

"Brennen?" Jaxcy watched him closely, seeing he seemed more rested.

"I'm fine, Jaxcy. And you?" He studied her before nodding. They would need to talk, he decided, but just how to approach her, that was the question. She was feeling guilty, of that, he had no doubt.

Later that afternoon, her hand tight in Brennen's, Kerry on his leash beside her, Jaxcy wandered some of the grounds and gardens with Brennen, awe on her face.

"This is huge!" Awe was on Jaxcy's face.

Brennen laughed. "It is. We are not far from Lake Erie. We'll walk there once we're better. I think Kerry might like to see the waves."

She glared at him for a moment. "Sure. Teach him to herd waves. We'll never keep him at home."

"No, we will. We'll make sure he's on a leash." Brennen's arm around her drew her close to him. "Now, Princess. I need to head for my office to see what I have waiting."

"I've taken you away from your work, haven't I?"

Brennen simply shook his head, walking her back to the building and in the back doors, to stop at an office door, unlocking it, and then reaching in to flick on the overhead lights.

Jaxcy stood in awe once more, spinning in a circle to study the rooms. Brennen reached to let Kerry off his leash, and the dog headed around the rooms, sniffing and familiarizing himself with them.

"Take all the time you need, Princess. I'll be in that room over there, checking my emails and whatnot." Brennen waited for a moment, not sure if she had heard him before he headed for his desk and was soon immersed in his work.

Looking up later, he found Jaxcy standing in front of him, uncertainty on her face. Not sure what was going on, he rose and headed around to her, drawing her into a hug, a grimace of pain crossing his face for a moment.

"What's wrong, Princess?"

Jaxcy finally answered. "I can't find the cleaning supplies. How do I clean your office if I can't?"

Brennen realized then that he had made a grievous error on not talking with Jaxcy, but then again, they had not had a lot of time to do so.

# Chapter 13

Brennen turned later that night, a mug of coffee in his hand, and leaned against the kitchen counter. He was exhausted, ready to sleep, but he needed time with God. He had no idea how to be a husband, how to protect Jaxcy. It didn't seem as if he had done that great already. Dallas had been by, just to update them and take what information they could give him, just to complete more of what he needed in the investigations. He had their statements, but he told them, things were remembered afterward.

Jaxcy had finally admitted that she thought that she had to clean the office and the apartment and do the laundry and cook. He had simply wrapped her into a hug and prayed for his princess. She kept looking at him as he called her that, but he had just shaken his head. She was not ready, not yet, to hear that she was the princess of his dreams, that he had fallen hard and fast for her.

She had shaken her own head when he told her that she didn't need to clean, that the Foundation had paid for years for housekeeping for the men, just as part of their mandate to be encouragers. When she had mentioned that she thought she had to, he had smiled and hugged her tighter. He told her that he had been looking after himself for years and that he didn't expect her to wait on him. They were partners, he stated, and would work together. She had protested that she had no training in anything else. Brennen had simply smiled, said that was okay, and that they would figure it out together, what she wanted to do. Right now, they both needed to heal.

Walking through the apartment, the lights low, he sighed to himself. He wanted this over, he thought. He knew it would only get worse and that scared him. He didn't want his Princess to be hurt her any more than she had been. He was in full realization that if he was hurt again, it would hurt her. He had seen something in her eyes that night as she had whispered a good night to him, something that gave him hope that just maybe she might, at some point, return his feelings.

He sat at his desk in his home office, pulling up his emails. He had not gotten too far that morning, and he knew the publisher he worked for had books waiting for him. He would need to work hard and long to catch up. He sent off the emails he needed to, took a quick look at the books waiting for him, his mind racing with the possibilities of what he could do, and then he turned to a search engine, searching for just what, he wasn't quite sure. He brought up news article after news article about Smithers, his face growing grimmer with each one.

Brennen finally sat back, exhaustion draining him, before he reached for his keyboard, sending off an email to a friend, asking her to search. A quick response startled him and then caused him to smile. Yes, he responded. He was having an adventure. No, he stated, he was not enjoying it, other than he had found his princess.

Startled, he looked up as he heard a noise, and then heard Kerry's low whine. He was on his feet, moving towards the bedroom, not finding Jaxcy. He began to panic, tracking Kerry's whine, finding the dog huddled down in the living room, protecting the door to the balcony.

"Kerry, what is it, boy? Where's our Princess?" Brennen dropped a hand on the dog's soft head as he stood, before he turned to search the living room, hearing soft sobs that he had not when he had entered. He approached Jaxcy, watching her closely, before he was on the floor beside her, gathering her to him,

Jaxcy pushed at him, bring a groan from him before his arms tightened. She pushed until she could push no longer, then collapsed against him, feeling his strength in how he held her, reading in it as well his feelings for her, and knowing that she was starting to love him, but she had decided it was too soon. She also quieted as she heard his prayer, before her eyes slid closed and she slept, her emotions and her physical injury stresses her body past its limits.

Brennen slept as well, unmindful of how hard the floor was. Kerry dropped his head on Brennen's leg and kept watch, growling as he heard a noise on the balcony, rising to stand at the door, his growl growing louder.

Jaxcy stirred late the next morning, feeling cold, a frown on her face as she realized that she was in Brennen's arms but that they were seated on the floor in the living room. She sighed. Another nightmare, she thought. She had not had one for weeks, but they were back. Kerry nudged at her, and she rose, heading to dress and then to take him outside. She didn't see Branigan and Buckley watching her or Brandon following her.

Brennen was at his desk when she returned, rising to greet her as she approached him.

"I'm sorry, Brennen. I had a nightmare."

"Did you? Do you have them often?" His arm around her, he walked them towards the living room.

"I haven't lately, but I used to have them every night." She sighed. "Kerry is upset about something."

"Is he?" Brennen had watched as Kerry had headed for the balcony door. "That's strange. Why is he at the door?"

"He kept wanting to go out there this morning. And just why did we sleep in the living room?"

"Because that is where I found you. You went to sleep and I couldn't lift you."

Jaxcy stared through the open door, seeing the package sitting there. "Brennen? What is that? It wasn't there last night."

"No, it wasn't." Brennen back away, shutting the door. "I need to call Dallas. He'll send someone out, I know. Meanwhile, let's get your tea and my coffee and head for my office."

Brennen looked up a couple of hours later as Dallas opened the door to his office and then entered, a shuttered look on his face as he stared at Jaxcy, who was ignoring him, engrossed as she was in a book. Rising, Brennen approached him.

"Dallas? I know that look."

Dallas nodded. "I know you do. Listen? Can we talk without Jaxcy being present?"

"Why?" Brennen felt Jaxcy's hand on his side.

"What is wrong? Why would you ask that?" Jaxcy's voice held a tinge of anger.

"Because of what was in that box. Did you place it there?" Dallas' voice was tight.

"What? How dare you accuse me of something like that?" Jaxcy's voice was barely audible as she spat her words out through her wired jaw before she ran, Kerry at her side, the door slamming behind her as much as any door in the building could slam.

Brennen glared at Dallas. "You had better have a good reason for this. I'm going after my wife. If I can convince her to return, we'll meet you in the conference room. If I can't, then we don't meet. I will not tolerate anyone treating or talking to her like this."

Dallas' hand went up as he opened his mouth to speak, but Brennen was gone before he could say a word. Dallas ran a hand through his hair. That went well, Lord. I let my anger and worry get the better of me. I know I shouldn't but these fellows have been through enough. He turned from the room, heading for the door, knowing he had other cases to work on but he really did need to talk to Brennen. He would return, hopefully before nightfall.

———

73

Brennen searched for Jaxcy, not finding her, not even finding Kerry, though he tried hard. Branigan and Brendon approached him, a frown on their faces, not quite sure what he was doing. Brennen turned as he heard his name, an arm wrapping around himself.

"Brennen? You look horrible!" Brendon's hand came out to steady his friend. "You should be inside, not out here. Not when it's about to rain."

"I can't find her."

"Who? Jaxcy? Is she out here with Kerry?" Branigan turned in a circle. "Where would they be?"

"That I don't know. She ran from my office, Kerry with her. Dallas was around. She didn't like that he accused her of placing a box on my balcony."

"A box? Wait! Brennen, what are you talking about?" Branigan looked up as others approached.

"There was a box placed on the balcony sometime overnight. Dallas retrieved it. We didn't get into what was in it. We didn't have a chance. He wanted to talk without Jaxcy present, she heard him, asked why and then ran." Brennen sighed. "I guess I wasn't too polite to him."

"It's understandable. Now, where would she have run to?" This from Benen.

"That I don't know. She's not familiar with the area. We walked through some of the gardens earlier but neither one of us was up to much. I'm afraid, fellows. Afraid that Smithers has her in his control."

"I just heard that Smithers has been found." Breck spoke from behind Brennen. "It's not good, fellows. He was found dead, shot."

"What?" Brennen spun, then struggled to keep his balance. "How?"

"That's what they're working on. Dallas called, looking for you. He's sending out a patrol car to provide some security for here until he can get more understanding of the situation. He has asked that we watch out for you two. Now, what is happening here?"

Buckley spoke up. "Jaxcy's missing. So is Kerry." He turned as he heard a sound and found Hagen and Devaney walking towards them.

"Hagen?" Brandon went towards his wife even as Blair headed towards Devaney.

"Where is Jaxcy? We found Kerry but we can't get him to rouse." Hagen pointed to the dog Devaney carried.

"Where?" Brennen was beside them, ready to head off to wherever it was he needed to be.

"By the roses. He was just laying there, Brennen. We didn't see Jaxcy and couldn't think of where she would be."

Brennen was away towards the garden before she had finished, not caring that his hurried movements

—

caused his pain to increase. He ignored it even as he searched for Jaxcy.

"She's not here, Brennen." Branigan's hand stopped his movements. "Come on. Back into the building. Breck called it in. Dallas is heading this way. It's getting dark."

"I know, but I need to find her. Where is she?" Brennen was beginning to panic.

The men shared looks and then spread out, Hagen and Devaney forcing Brennen to go with him, using the fact that Kerry was hurt and that Jaxcy would want him to look after the dog.

An hour later, Brennen still sat in the lobby area of the building, the heat from one gas fireplace not warming him. He cradled Kerry in his arms, the dog awake and alert, but not willing to leave Brennen. There had been no reports yet that Jaxcy had been found. It was dark now, with a misty rain falling, chilling the searchers.

Barnabas halted beside Brody. "No sign?"

"Not yet. I don't like this, Barnabas. Too many of us have disappeared from here."

"I know, Brody, but we can't fence it off. Dallas said he was heading for Jaxcy's property in the event she might be there."

"As if she'd be in the open. I'm not sure that she evens knows which area is hers."

"No, I don't think she does. Brennen said he hadn't talked to her about that yet." Barnabas frowned as he heard a soft sound. "Did you hear that?"

"I did." Brody spun, before pointing. "That way, I think." He was off on a run, following the faint sounds that came his way. He slid to a halt, a hand out to stop Barnabas. "In here, somewhere, Barnabas. If it's Jaxcy, she can't yell."

Barnabas hesitated, his head tilted to listen, before he was reaching for the bushes, parting them, an exclamation drawn from him. "Jaxcy!"

Brody pushed past him, dropping to his knees, his hand reaching for his pocket knife, to slash the bonds that had held her prisoner. "Jaxcy?" When she barely nodded, he was pulling off his jacket, to wrap it around her before he rose, Jaxcy in his arms. "We need to get her to Doc."

"We do. You're okay?" Barnabas held the bushes back once more before he headed almost on a run for the building, Brody following at a rapid pace.

"I am. She's freezing, though."

The men headed directly to the infirmary, finding Doc walking towards them.

"Brody? You found her?" Doc had the door open and the lights on in the room, heading for where he had left his stethoscope.

Brody was away, looking for Cadee, who was training as a nurse, knowing Doc would want her help. Anna was already heading his way.

"Brody? I just heard. Have you found her?"

"We have, Anna. In the infirmary. I was looking for Cadee." He paused, not sure which way to go.

Anna simply reached to hug him, turning him to walk back with her. "Benen will find her. The ladies were heading for the chapel, to spend time in prayer." Anna watched her young friend, a frown puckering her forehead for a moment. Something is going on with Brody, Lord, and I am not sure what. The fellows are feeling the stress of the last months and into years, not sure who would be next. Please, dear Lord, walk with each one. Guide their steps. Help us to intercede on their behalf. Before we even speak, You have heard and answered.

# Chapter 15

Cadee approached Jaxcy's bedside during the night, her hand reaching for her stethoscope. Doc, Anna, and she had worked frantically to warm Jaxcy, Doc sending Cadee to find Brennen and then sending her to find warm dry clothes for the younger woman. Jaxcy had not roused at all, the chill coming from her worrying Doc. He had not said much, simply shook his head, started an IV, and then asked for hot water bottles and heavy blankets, to try and warm her. It had finally succeeded, the blue of her lips fading to normal pink.

Cadee's gaze shifted to Brennen, who slept on the stretcher that Blair and Burnie had wheeled in, refusing to leave Jaxcy, simply shaking his head. Brennen had refused to state what he thought, that somehow Smithers was still alive, that Dallas had been wrong, and that Smithers would somehow make his way to find her and take her somewhere Brennen could not find her.

Brennen had roused as he heard Cadee moving around, opening his eyes to a small crack, watching Jaxcy. His thoughts drifted to the night before, when Breck had found him in the lobby. Breck had dropped to a seat beside him, after he had taken off his jacket, frowning at the ice crystals that had formed.

"We found her, Brennen." Breck's hand kept Brennen in his seat. "Wait. We need to talk before you go to her. Barnabas and Brody found her. She was found, lying in some bushes. With the rain now turning to sleet, she would not have survived overnight. Doc, Anna, and Cadee are with her. Brady here will stay with you for now." Breck had shaken his head at Brennen's protest. "He stays. Dallas caught up with me. With the sleet moving in and changing to heavier ice, he won't be out tonight. He's not sure when he will be able to get out. He did ask that I talk to you. He sends his apologies."

"Yeah, well, about that. He needs to apologize to Jaxcy. I won't have her accused of a crime." Brennen's look was mutinous.

"He knows that and he feels bad. That's no excuse that he doesn't know her. She's the innocent party in all this."

"He left a voice mail for me, telling me that there was a direct threat against me in that box. It held pictures of me over the last week and from when I was at Jaxcy's. Someone is following me." Brennen rose, staring down at Breck. "Again, she is not the culprit here. I don't know who is." He turned and walked rapidly away, not looking back.

Brandon shared a look with Blair before he spoke. "He's right. She is the innocent party in this. So is he. If it's not Smithers, then who is it?"

"He had to be working for someone. He never had a traceable source of income, not that we can determine." Barnabas spoke from behind them. "How be we spend some time in prayer for our friends and then try to get some work done?" He squinted at his watch. "It's early yet. Unless you have plans?"

"No, none of us. The ladies are in the chapel, praying. We can work." Buckley strode away, heading for the conference room, following by the others.

Watching Cadee leave, Brennen hesitated before he rose, a prayer rising within him, a prayer for healing, for peace, for wisdom, for resolution of this that they found themselves in. He cried out for protection for his princess, knowing that the day before could have turned out so differently.

He stood, his hand on her cheek, wincing at the fading bruising, anger burning within him. He wanted revenge on whoever had done this, whoever had been behind Smithers. Then, he grew repentant. Vengeance was God's, not his. He breathed a sigh, his eyes closing as he surrendered his will, once more, and surrendered his Princess to God.

Jaxcy stirred, her eyes opening as she awakened, searching the dimly-lit room. The hospital again? She closed her eyes, a deep breath trying to calm her agitation. She felt the hand on her cheek and turned into it, recognizing Brennen's touch, even though their touches had been minimal to that point. She searched his face, seeing the peace that he was obtaining starting to flood it. She raised a hand to touch his, bringing a smile to his face as he opened his eyes.

"Princess? How are you?" He leaned closer to her.

"Sore. Where am I? The hospital?"

"No, in the infirmary in our building. You had an adventure and didn't take me with you."

"I did? I'm sorry. Dallas, was it?" At his nod, she sighed once more. "I need to apologize. I let my fear and anger speak and then drive me away."

"He wants to apologize to you as well. He realized that he didn't approach it correctly."

"I'm not used to interacting with people. I only saw a few on Sundays when I could get out to church, or if I had to shop, which was only every four to six weeks."

"No excuse for his anger. He told me that he was afraid for us." Brennen dropped the bed rail, and then sitting beside her, cradled her to him. "I can see his point."

"True, but what was in that box?"

"Pictures of me. Threats." He looked down. "I have some news. Smithers was murdered."

"He was?" Jaxcy twisted to look at him. "But that doesn't mean it's over, does it?"

"No, it doesn't. Barnabas was around late last night, just to see how we were doing. The fellows have started their investigation. They've become pros at this, seeing as I am the ninth to have an adventure."

"Nine? That's a lot. And it won't end until we get to Barnabas, now will it?" Jaxcy shifted once more. "Kerry?"

"He's at home. He was hurt, but Brady took a look at him. He doesn't think he was hurt too bad."

"I tried to stop the man from hitting him. He just shoved me away and when Kerry was down, he came after me. I tried to fight him off but he was too strong. He tied me up and dumped me in some bushes." Jaxcy stared down at her clasped hands. "I'm sorry, Brennen. I'm so sorry."

"It's okay, Princess. It's okay. You're here and safe." Brennen's arm tightened on her.

"Take me home, Brennen. I need to go home."

The tears and pleas in her voice broke his heart. Without saying a word, he simply gathered her into his arms, heading for their apartment, and then wrapping her in a blanket, dropped into his favourite armchair and sat, his head on hers as they both slept.

# Chapter 16

Standing at his kitchen counter, his focus on the scenery he could see outside of the window above the sink, Brennen listened as Branigan, Brendon, and Breck discussed what they had discovered. He shuddered at what they were saying, how Smithers had been behind so much destruction and devastation in the area. He knew only too well how he had worked. Both Brennen and Jaxcy had been his victims, Jaxcy more so than he had been.

He turned, his mug of tea in his hand. Staring down at it, he wondered when tea had become his beverage of choice and not the coffee he loved. He sighed, setting down his mug, and walking away from the men, leaving Breck staring after him for a moment.

Brennen stopped in the hallway, his eyes on Jaxcy as she stood, arms wrapped around herself, unwilling to enter the kitchen. She looked up at him, her eyes huge in her pale face, the effects of the chill from the day before still there. He simply reached to wrap her in his arms, his embrace tightening as he felt the sobs starting, sorrow in his heart for her. He stood, hearing footsteps behind him that paused.

"Princess? What's wrong?" He finally spoke, not sure if she would even respond.

"Take me home, Brennen. Please?"

"You are home, Princess. This is our home." Brennen was puzzled.

"No, take me home. To my cabin. I want to go back there. I felt safe there. Here I don't." Her sobs deepened.

"Princess? Do you want to go back there? It's not safe for you there. Breck is here. He has information about the law and the townspeople that he needs to talk to you about." Brennen was unable to reach through her distress, finally just scooping her into his arms and heading for his chair in the kitchen, a quiet thank you to Breck who pulled it back.

The three men watched as Jaxcy's tears were finally spent, and she just laid back against Brennen, not saying anything.

"Brennen?" Branigan finally spoke, breaking the silence.

"She wants to go back to her cabin. And we know that's not safe. And it doesn't seem to be any safer here. So what do we do?" Brennen felt awkward, even asking that.

"We keep you both here. Your work is here. You are both exhausted in more ways than one. Jaxcy has been thrust into a building and among people she doesn't know. She has not had a chance to relax or recover. That's something that preys on her feelings. You two were married without being able to discuss it or even truly agree to it. She stepped in to save you, Brennen. She will have questions as to whether she did what was right."

Jaxcy had looked up at Branigan was speaking, finally nodding. "All that and more." She was frustrated that her wired-together jaw kept her from talking a lot. Brendon finally shoved a pad of paper and his pen towards her, finding himself the object of her intense regard before she nodded and took the pen, her fingers forcing it to fly across the paper as she filled and then turned page after page. The four men watched her closely, not sure of what she was thinking.

Finally pushing the papers towards Breck, Jaxcy sank back against Brennen, exhausted, and suddenly realizing he still held her. Her head tilted back to study him, finding his eyes on her, a compassionate look on his face before he nodded.

"So, what do we have here, Jaxcy?" Breck spoke as he gathered the papers and looked them over, a shocked look on his face as he looked back up at her. "Jaxcy? You're sure about this?"

She nodded. "I am. I want this wire out now." She was frustrated at not being able to speak correctly.

"Not for a week or so, Princess. That's what the surgeon said. If we take it out too soon, you won't heal properly."

Branigan had been reading her notes and looked up, surprise on his face. "Jaxcy, this bit about Smithers' family. Do you know them?"

"I guess. I never connected them with him. I know the name is the same. Why?"

"Because we came across those very names last night when we were researching. They seem to have traveled back and forth between here and your town." Branigan handed the pages over to Brendon.

"When was that law set up?" Brendon's mind had taken off on a tangent.

"Twelve years ago, I think. I'm not sure." Jaxcy paled. "It was around the time that my parents died." She twisted to stare at Brennen. "Brennen? I never got an accident report. I was just told it was a landslide."

"And you think now that maybe it wasn't just an accident?" Brennen nodded. "I have been wondering that. We can't get those reports. Dallas has tried and been denied."

"The next step would be Emma, wouldn't it?" Breck pulled out his phone. "I'll call her. I have the information here." He was on his feet, walking away, leaving Jaxcy staring after him.

"What did he say?"

"We have a friend who is very good at finding information that no one else can. He's calling her to get her started on the search." Brennen sighed as his phone rang and he pulled it out. "Emma? She's sent an email."

# Chapter 17

Late that night, Brennen sat back from his computer. He was feeling physically better, he thought, but he was worried about Jaxcy. She had been quiet, quieter than she was normally. When he had approached her, she had just shaken her head, said she was tired and walked away, Kerry standing watching her before he turned to Brennen.

He had a handle on what work he needed to do, and the ideas were flowing. He sighed. As much as he wanted to work on the investigation, at present he had obligations to his publisher. He hadn't realized that he had so much work outstanding.

Walking through the low-lit apartment, Brennen studied it, trying to see it from Jaxcy's point of view once more. He just couldn't. He couldn't get past the huge contrast and that worried him. He was afraid she would just pack up and leave him, overwhelmed with her new life. His prayer was that he could reach her and help her. At the present time, he was just not sure how he could.

Standing in the living room doorway, Jaxcy watched Brennen, realizing that she had come to love him, but too unsure of herself to approach him. She finally walked towards him, sitting beside him, her hands clasped on her lap. She didn't speak, not wanting to disturb him, just in case he was praying.

Brennen tilted his head to study Jaxcy, not saying anything, his hand resting on Kerry's head. He finally spoke, talking about his life in foster care, how he had never known his parents and had always wondered what they would have been like. Jaxcy's eyes were on his face, sympathy on hers.

"You never knew them?"

Brennen shook his head. "I don't, I don't think. I was only two or three when I was taken into custody and placed in foster care. I have tried to find out why, but the records have been sealed by the courts. I have put in a petition through the lawyers here to have them unsealed, but we are still waiting."

"That's so sad." She looped an arm around his, laying her head on his shoulder. "I had mine. We had our disagreements as all families did, but I knew they loved me." She paused, a thread of thought catching at the edge of her mind. "Do you think this Emma will find out something?"

"I am sure that she will. She's good. The best in the business is what I have heard."

"Then, that's how we pray. I am tired of living like I am. I want stability."

"You have that with me, Princess. No matter what we go through, I am not walking away from you." He turned to face her. "I heard from Dallas earlier."

"And?" She looked up at him. "What did he want?"

"Just to let me know that they have the man in custody who shot Smithers. It was unrelated to our adventure, he said, but that we needed to be extremely careful. They are sorting through all the paperwork they found in his office. He has contacts that are still dangerous to us. In fact, Dallas said he had put out a contract on us. He was wanting revenge."

"Did we ever find out what happens to the property if I die after I was married?"

Brennen nodded. "It still goes to a trust, but this time it goes to a trust that can't be transferred or broken. It is to fund high school scholarships."

"Wow! Who set that up?"

"Burnie was working on that, along with Blair. They're searching through all sorts of dummy companies and whatnot."

"So that may not even be true. Who owned the property, to begin with?"

"That's what we can't determine." Brennen sighed. "I'm sorry. There doesn't seem to be many answers for you."

"It is just so strange. Why me? What did my parents ever do to have this come down on me?"

Brennen raised a finger to halt her words, a thought running through his mind. "What did your parents do?"

"What do you mean, what did they do?"

"For a living, occupation, whatever you want to call it."

"Dad? He was a police officer. Mom stayed home. She was a proofreader for technical manuals. Do you think that this is it?"

Brennen nodded. "We have not looked closely at your parents, at least, I don't think so. Maybe it was revenge for your parents or something." He groaned as his phone chimed and he twirled it on the coffee table to look at it. "Emma. She's sent an email that she needs us to look at right away."

"She does that?"

"She does." Brennen stood, reaching for Jaxcy's hand, pulling her to the office with him, before he shoved her into his desk chair, pulling up another beside her. "Let's see what she has to say."

Jaxcy was confused. She knew about emails and stuff like that, she thought, but she had never used them herself. Brennen failed to see the look on her face at first until he turned to speak.

"I'm sorry, Princess. I'm just so used to this. Here. Let me explain. You have heard about emails and email addresses?" At her nod, he continued. "Emma has sent an email and has attached documents that she wants us to look at. I'll put them up, print them and then we can look them over."

"That's a lot of work." Jaxcy tried to protest at him doing that.

"Not at all. I'll need to print them anyway, I suspect, for the fellows." He was on his feet, retrieving the papers before he was back to his desk, in his chair, finding Jaxcy reaching for the stack. "Jaxcy?"

"I can at least sort it for you. How many copies?"

"I did six. One for each of us. One for Dallas. And then three for the fellows. They'll copy them as they need to." He reached for the copies, stacking them neatly before he turned to her. "Now, we take our highlighters, pens, and whatever, head to the living room or kitchen, wherever you wish, and work away."

"It's late, Brennen."

"I know, but neither one of us will rest easy until this is over. I want it over yesterday. You need it over."

"I do." She sighed. "I just don't get why God has allowed this. I'm not someone who would have chosen this."

"I know, Princess. I know. Let's pray first and then we'll find a late-night snack to tide us over."

*Chapter 18*

Late the next morning, Brennen looked up at a tap at his office door and watched as Dallas entered. Dallas was on a search for the couple, needing to speak with them.

"Jaxcy?"

"She's with the ladies, at Anna's. Do you need to speak with her?" Brennen dropped the pencil he had been holding. "I can get her."

"Not right away. I do want to speak with her, apologize, and then update her. But, you. What did you go and do, Brennen?" Dallas spoke half in jest.

"I don't understand." Brennen was puzzled, pointing to a chair for Dallas to sit.

"I received a raft of material from Emma and then from the Foundation lawyer. They have been researching you. The lawyer has finally been able to unseal the court records concerning you. He said he had tried to call you this morning."

Brennen groaned. "I always mute my phone when I am working." He reached for it, accessing his voice mail, wonder growing on his face as he listened to the lawyer's message. He set his phone down carefully before he looked at Dallas.

"Did you know?"

—

"Know what? That you were an orphan, that your mother gave you up because she was dying from cancer. That your father had been killed in a road rage incident before you were born?"

"That. I never knew." Brennen sat back, his hands rubbing at his face, blowing out a deep breath. "I never imagined that, you know. He said he has pictures and other things for me, including a letter from my mother."

"That's interesting. I would like to know why it was never given to you before."

"He's looking into that. He has approached the powers that be down there and is raising a ruckus, as he put it." Brennen looked down, overcome for a moment. "Now, about Jaxcy?"

"About Jaxcy. Can we go find her? That way, I only have to talk once." Dallas grinned at Brennen.

"Sure. I'm not sure exactly where she is." Brennen held up a hand. "And no, she has refused a phone. She admitted that she is somewhat scared of the phones nowadays."

"That's interesting. I wouldn't have thought that." Dallas followed Brennen down the hallway.

"She is quiet, not saying a lot of what bothers her. She has been beaten down by life and just trying to survive. I have to pull things from her, although she is getting better at talking with me."

Jaxcy looked up from where she has seated on Anna's couch, Fynn and Ennis on either side of her. She went to rise but Brennen motioned for her to stay put. He headed for the kitchen, Dallas in tow, and she heard his laughter as Anna teased him.

Fynn rose as Brennen approached, moving to let him sit beside Jaxcy, a word to Anna as she left, an eye on her watch. The other ladies gradually found their way out, calling back to Jaxcy that they had enjoyed themselves and they wanted to meet every week, if she would let them.

Brennen wrapped an arm around her, feeling the fatigue as she leaned against him. Knowing that she would not say a word, he smiled.

"Overdid it, did they?" He grinned at her frown. "They don't understand, Princess, how it is with you. You aren't used to being around people. I can talk to them or you can."

"You can't!" Jaxcy was horrified at the thought of him doing just that. Then she looked over at Dallas. "I need to apologize, Dallas. I let my temper get the best of me and I should have stayed and listened to what you had to say. It has been a while since you have been here."

Dallas grinned. "It has been. Apology accepted. I need to apologize as well. I shouldn't have approached our last meeting as I did. That being said, I do need to talk with you both."

Brennen spoke up, his eyes on Jaxcy. "It's okay, Jaxcy. I have some stuff to talk to you about, but we'll do that later. Right now, Dallas has some information that he needs to tell us."

"I do." Dallas opened the folder he had been carrying with him. He handed over some photos, watching Jaxcy closely as she took them. "Do you know these men?"

She stared at him for a full moment before her eyes dropped. She nodded. "This one? The gray-haired man? He's the mayor of my town. He has been for twenty years or so. No one has ever run against him. This second photo? That's his brother. He's the town accountant. The next one? He's the chief of police. The next one? That's the town's attorney. The minister and I suspected that they were all involved in drafting and ramming through the law. Does that make sense?"

"It does. Considering the law came on the books just before your parents died? We think it was directly to target you." Dallas looked down, discomfort and sorrow on his face, before he looked back at Jaxcy. "I'm sorry, Jaxcy. Your parents did not die in a landslide. It was made to look like that. We brought in the provincial police force, who have now taken over the enforcement in your town. The four men? They are under arrest. Thanks to the Foundation lawyer and friends he has in high places down there, we have been able to pull some records. With your permission, we would like to exhume your parents' bodies and have a medical examiner from outside the area do a new autopsy. In fact, there was never one done. It was blocked by the police chief."

"That's what I could never understand. They just told me that they were dead. They wouldn't even allow me to see their bodies. They sealed the caskets at the funeral. I protested, the minister and his wife protested, but they didn't allow it. They gave some flimsy reason." She blinked rapidly to dispel the tears. "How do I even know it was them? I never saw them. I only had their word it was my parents. How do I know for sure that it was? Will this examination prove that?"

# Chapter 19

Two weeks later, Brennen stepped back from the apartment door, his eyes on Dallas and then Barnabas as they entered. Something was up, of that he was sure. He had been out and about, feeling that he was being followed, but not seeing anyone that he could pinpoint.

"Dallas?" Brennen pointed to the living room. "I'll get Jaxcy."

"Just a moment, Brennen, before you do. We need to talk to both of you, but it is mostly what we have found about her parents." Dallas shook his head at Brennen's questioning look.

Jaxcy hesitated as she approached before Brennen reached to sweep her close to him. She was puzzled at the comment that she had overheard.

"Dallas?"

"Jaxcy? How are you?" Dallas grinned for a moment before he sobered. "I have news, Jaxcy. Can we sit?"

She shrugged. "I guess. I don't know why everyone wants to sit when it's bad news."

"Perhaps so that their legs don't give out and they end up in a heap on the floor." Barnabas grinned at her in turn. He waited until they were seated before he prayed, knowing that what Dallas had to say would be disturbing, to say the least.

"Dallas? What news do you have?" Brennen waited, his hand clasped tightly by both of Jaxcy's.

"Jaxcy, we have a report back on the landslide and then from the medical examiner. It has been determined that the landslide was deliberate but that the people in the car were not killed by it. They were dead already when the landslide hit the car."

Jaxcy paled. "Dead? Before? But how?"

"They were shot, according to the report. The bullets were still in the coffins. No one did an examination on them at all." Dallas paused, his eyes on Brennen before he looked at Jaxcy. "Now, according to the report, the people would have been in their mid-thirties."

"That can't be right. Mom and Dad would have been in their forties. I don't understand." She looked between Brennen and Dallas, a bewildered look on her face, not seeing how Barnabas was watching her.

"I think that it means that they weren't your parents. Is that correct, Dallas?" Brennen spoke up, wanting to change it for his princess but unable to.

"That is correct. They were both males. The force is looking into that, and say charges are pending."

"The mayor?"

"That is who they suspect. Now, as to your parents? We can find no evidence that they are dead. Where they are? That is the question. We have expanded our search to outside of Newfoundland, to across the country, and even into the States."

“What? You mean they may still be alive? But how?” Jaxcy was even more confused.

“That is what we don’t know. We’re still digging into records and conducting interviews. We’re still a long way from where we need to be.”

Jaxcy nodded, a saddened look on her face. “They are dead, Dallas. I don’t doubt that. I would suggest you search his property outside of town. It’s a large forested area. There have always been rumours about bodies that he had buried there.”

Dallas nodded. “We have heard those too. There will be cadaver dogs going in to search. I’m sorry, Jaxcy. I was hoping to put this to rest for you.”

“It is what it is.” Jaxcy hesitated and then rose, walking away, only Brennen seeing the tears on her face.

“Excuse me.” Brennen was on his feet, following her, reaching to wrap her into his arms, holding her as she sobbed. He knew that the investigation had opened wounds that hadn’t healed. He had no idea what to say or even if he should say anything. He just prayed for his princess, asking for healing for her. “You okay, sweetheart?” He finally broke into the storm of tears.

“I don’t know. I just don’t know.” She frowned at him. “Brennen? Why that word?”

“What word?”

“Sweetheart. You always call me Princess and that I don’t even understand.”

Brennen hugged her tighter. “You are the princess of my dreams, the one I was waiting for all my life. And you are my sweetheart. I never knew when the time would be right. This is not likely it, but I just wanted you to know that I love you, more each day."

Jaxcy stared at him, finally remembering to snap her mouth closed. "You do?" Her voice was barely audible. "Oh, Brennen. I was so afraid. Afraid that you would never care for me. I thought you were only doing what you were because you thought you had to as a husband. Taking care of me, making sure I was okay."

"That's part of it." Brennen looked towards the doorway of the office. "I need to go back and talk to those two. But understand this. Our conversation is not over. Not by a long shot. Stay here. I'll talk to them, see what else they can tell me."

The three men talked for a while longer before they rose. Brennen shut the door behind them, standing with a hand braced against it, suddenly unsure of himself. And that was not like him, he knew. He felt Jaxcy's hand on his back and turned suddenly, just sweeping her to his heart and kissing her. They had to talk, they both knew, but their mutually discovered love was too new and fresh to disturb it with words.

# Chapter 20

A week later, Jaxcy curled up in the large easy chair that Brennen had found and moved into his office. He wanted her near him, he said. She had laughed, shaken her head, and then circled it. She needed to find something constructive to do, she knew, but just what that was, she wasn't sure. Brennen had gladly let her have a sketch pad, bought her the pencils she refused to ask for, and left her to sketch.

Brennen looked up after a time, finding Jaxcy intent on her work, a pencil between her lips, another stuck behind her ear, her face a study in concentration. Who knew, he thought, that he would find a bride who liked to draw as well? God was in that, he knew. He had to be.

He looked towards the door as a tap came to it and then Brady peeked around it, beckoning Brennen to come outside. Brennen rose, a glance thrown towards Jaxcy before he closed the door behind him.

"Brady?"

"Brennen, we have found something in our research. We need to talk to you about it. It concerns your parents."

"And? I have a deadline I'm working on. I have to have the sketches in today." He frowned. "Can I have a couple of hours?"

"Sure. Come and find us when you're done."

Brennen watched Brady walk away before he shook his head and then returned to his work, the illustrations coming to life under his fingers. He felt Jaxcy's hand on his shoulder as he finished and sat back, an arm out to sweep her to his lap, his kiss on her lips stilling her protest.

"Brennen? What did Brady want? You were so deep in your concentration when you came back that I didn't want to disturb you."

"Thank you, Princess. He needs to talk to me. Something about my parents. And no, I will not let you stay away. You're going with me." He reached around her to the keyboard. "I just need to save these and then send them on. There. Another book done."

"Just like that? They're gone?" Jaxcy was always surprised at the speed at which the emails traveled back and forth.

"They are." Brennen reached to kiss her again, hearing Kerry whining at his feet. "It's okay, Kerry. We are not ignoring you, now are we?" He laughed as Jaxcy playfully swatted at him.

Jaxcy watched him, waiting for him to move, but he seemed to be content just to sit and hold her. And she was content to be held. "Brennen? Don't we need to go find Brady?"

"We do. I guess that means we have to get up?"

"It does." Jaxcy slipped from his knee, her hand held out for him. She was becoming more accustomed to showing her emotions with him, although she struggled at times. "Dallas was around when you were deep in concentration."

"He was? I didn't know that. How did I miss him?"

"It was when I had Kerry outside. And no, I was not on my own. Eric followed me." She sighed. "Dallas needs to talk to us too at some point over the next couple of days. He warned me to be extra cautious right now. Whoever it is that they are looking at, he said, is in the area and word on the street, as he put it, is that they are looking for us."

"That's what they always do. Put out a contract on the couple. It's what happened with the others." Brennen locked the office door and reached for her hand, heading for the other hallway and the conference room. "Listen. We need to go out for a dinner. Dress up, if you wish."

"Dress up? I don't know, Brennen. It's been so long."

"I know it has, Princess, but we'll work on it. We'll just take what time you need."

"Thank you, love. Now, are we going in or are we just going to stand out here?" She was becoming freer in how she teased him, his love, and confidence in her bringing more confidence to her.

"Going in, I guess." He opened the door and waited until she entered, his eyes searching the faces that turned their way. All of them were there, including Barnabas. And Dallas, as well. This can't be good, he thought.

“Brady? You wanted to talk to us?”

“We did. Here.” Brady was on his feet, heading for the coffee that was on and then heading for Brennen and Jaxcy, their coffee and tea mugs in his hands. “Sit. This is going to take a while.”

“That doesn’t sound good.” Brennen sighed. “How long has it been, fellows? And how soon can we have it over?”

# Chapter 21

Rising from where she had been sitting, Jaxcy moved around the room, her mind whirling at the information being thrown at them. She turned to face the room, leaning back into a corner, a hand rubbing at her temple. She still suffered from headaches on occasions, and this was one of those, she thought.

Fynn approached her, a mug of tea extended. "How are you, Jaxcy?"

"To tell you the truth, I really don't know. I don't know how I am to be. There is just so much." She nodded towards the men. "How do they do this? They just absorb it and continue, new questions, ideas, and thoughts flying at each other."

"That's how they work. They have been friends for so long, they really do understand to a degree how each one thinks. What one doesn't think of, the other does." Fynn grinned. "Anna maintains that it is a good thing they are not small boys. They would be in constant trouble."

Jaxcy smiled at that. "I can see that. They like to tease and torment each other, as my mother would have said." She paused, a sad look crossing her face. "I talked to Dallas a while ago, when he came back. He didn't have good news for me."

"Oh, no! Your parents?"

Jaxcy nodded. "They still have not found any sign of them. He said he talked to my minister and his wife, but they were not much help. Whatever happened to them, it has been well hidden." She sighed a deeper sigh. "This has been so hard, you know? Marrying as we did. Moving here. It is such a contrast."

"Talk to me, Jaxcy. Here. Let's go sit in the lobby. Some of the other ladies are around. Do you mind if they join us?"

Jaxcy stared at her for a moment, shocked. "You really mean that?"

"I do. Oh, Jaxcy! Did you think we didn't want to know you, knowing that you had little in your life, that you had had to scrimp and scrape to get by? That's not it. We just weren't sure if you were ready to be inundated with our friendship."

"I would like that friendship. It's just been hard. I wasn't around people a lot in the last few years. I just couldn't."

Fynn reached to hug Jaxcy, before she pointed to the door. "Let's head out there." She waved at Brennen as he stood watching them. "Brennen knows you are with me."

"He does? Okay."

An hour later, Brennen stood where he could watch the ladies, without being seen. He frowned as he watched Jaxcy, seeing that she was trying hard to join in but showed to him that she was overwhelmed.

Brady nodded towards the ladies. "Your lady? You need to rescue her from my lady. Fynn sometimes doesn't get the personal touch that she needs to have, particularly if someone doesn't stand up to her. She's trying, but she's used to dealing with creepy-crawlies."

Brennen grinned. "That she is. I know I need to go rescue her, but I don't want to interfere if that is how she would see it."

Brady simply shook his head, walked across the lobby to the ladies, and scooped Fynn into his arms, sitting back where she had been. Fynn let out a squeal, bringing laughter from most of the ladies, but a shocked look from Jaxcy that she quickly covered.

Brennen crouched down beside her chair, an arm around her.

"Having fun, Princess?"

Jaxcy turned to him, seeing his concern for her in his eyes. "I am, but I need to leave, Brennen. How do I do that? I know Dallas needs to talk to us."

He dropped a kiss on her temple. "It's very easy. You stand up, excuse yourself, and walk away hand in hand with me."

She stared at him, shocked, then rose as he tugged at her hand as he stood.

"If you will excuse us, ladies, Brady, Jaxcy and I need to go find Dallas before he thinks we have run away." He waved at their laughter, not seeing their concern as they watched Jaxcy.

"She's really hurting." Ennis commented.

"She is. I notice that she had become quieter as time went on." Hagen sighed. "I think it was too much."

"Not too much, Hagen." Brady spoke up. "It's that she has never really had a close friend, from what Brennen said when he asked for prayer for her. And I am not betraying a confidence when I say that. He has given permission for us to talk to our ladies. And going through what she has now? The uncertainty about her parents? That is hard on her."

"And she has only finished high school. The rest of us have some college education or university education. She likely feels inadequate based on that." Cadee blinked to clear away the tears she refused to shed, thinking of what it must be like for Jaxcy. "She reminds me of the ladies and girls I worked with in the mission."

"Then, how do we reach her, Cadee?" Berneen leaned forward. "We need to do that. It breaks my heart to think of this."

Brady had been listening. "My advice? Just be yourselves. Be her friend. Include her when she is willing. Let her have her space. Cadee, didn't your parents say they wanted to start a garden at the shelter? Then include her with that. That was how she had her food. She grew it."

# Chapter 22

Dallas watched Brennen closely as he seated Jaxcy at the table that he had taken over, spreading out his documents and notes. Jaxcy rubbed her hands along her legs, nervous for a moment, her eyes on the paperwork.

"Dallas? Where do we start?" Brennen sat, knowing that the room had quieted for them.

"Let's spend some time in prayer first, if you don't mind. I need it, and I know you two do as well."

Finally looking up, Brennen kept his eyes on Jaxcy.

"What do you have, Dallas?"

"For starters, your minister friend, Jaxcy, is a wealth of information, information that he really didn't know he had. The skilled investigators have pulled it from him. And the police force in your town has been disbanded for now as has the town council. The mayor and the police chief are under arrest. The plan is to set up a new council and a new police force, using some of the same men and women who were on the force."

"That's good. They weren't all bad." Jaxcy leaned against Brennen. "But, where does that leave us?"

"Sitting at a table, trying to make sense of everything?" Dallas grinned at her. "Seriously, it does move the investigation along. There are some things that I can't discuss with you.

"First, your parents. The land belonging to the mayor has been searched. The cadaver dogs made no hits, which was good in a sense. They are moving on to other properties."

Jaxcy nodded, a thought crossing her mind. "Could my parents still be alive? I know it has been a lot of years. Could they?"

"That is a possibility we are strongly looking at. I can't go into those details at the moment. Have you thought of anyone, anything else that you can tell me?"

Jaxcy shook her head. "I have had 11 years or so to do just that. Think. Not to think. To avoid people because of the looks of pity sent my way. To avoid people because of the anger directed at me, the hate, the physical abuse. Why, Dallas? Why did they do this?"

"That is what I needed to talk to you about. The trust fund? It comes from your parents. Even if they had been alive, it still would have come to you. It is money that they received as inheritances that they pooled into a trust fund for you. They tried to keep it a secret, but the banker talked and that's how this all started.

"The law in town? That was set up specifically directed at you. They wanted you to avoid marriage, to stay out of touch with people, to keep to yourself. Every young man in town, who had remained, was warned to stay away from you, or they would be jailed for some reason."

Jaxcy looked at Dallas in horror, Brennen's arm around her to comfort her.

"They did that? All to get my money? I don't want it. What can I do with it?" She swiped at the tears on her cheeks, not willing to acknowledge them, but knowing she had to wipe them away.

"We can discuss that later, Princess." Brennen pointed to the paper that Dallas was holding out for her. "Dallas needs you to take that."

Jaxcy reached a tentative hand to take it, turning it to read it, shock on her face. "There is that much?"

"There is. You are a wealthy young lady. It may not seem like much, but it would be enough to keep you for life, if you use it frugally. If you had still been at your own home, you would not have had to scrimp and save and scrape to get by."

Brennen tilted Jaxcy's hand to read the financial paper, then bent his head to study her.

"Jaxcy? We don't have to decide anything today."

"I know. I just don't get it. We never had a lot when I was small. We had enough to get by with, with some left over." She looked up at him. "They did this for me?"

"They did." Dallas handed over other papers. "These go with that. Now, as to Smithers? He was not the main person, the main one responsible. He had heard of the trust fund, how we are still tracking through the web of deceit that he wove. But he did have contacts there, shall we say of the unsavoury kind?

How he found out about this? Likely by someone talking that shouldn't have. The investigators are appalled at how the information has been noised around town."

"And if Mom and Dad were gone, and I didn't marry, or marry too late, it went to Smithers?"

"That's what they have tried to say, what paperwork you were given at some point said. Where did it come from?"

Jaxcy stared at him and then felt anger growing in her. "The banker. How is he related to Smithers?"

"I like how you think. Brennen, she went right to the heart of the matter, something that took us a while to figure out. He is a cousin of Smithers."

"But who killed him?" Jaxcy turned to study Brennen. "Someone did. And why?"

"That we are working on." Dallas sighed. "I know that I keep saying that, Jaxcy, but that is how investigations work. We nibble away at information, trying to connect it, praying that it will be over soon. Sometimes it is. Sometimes it isn't." He groaned as his phone rang and he pulled it out. "Excuse me. I have to take this call. I will be back."

Brennen watched him walk away before he spoke, his eyes connecting with Branigan.

"Jaxcy? Are you okay with all this?"

She shrugged. "I have no idea. It's just so much information." She frowned as she read a portion of one of the papers. "This is not right, Brennen. This lists Dad's family. He was not an only child. He had two siblings, a brother and a sister. His sister? I knew her. She moved out to British Columbia when I was about ten or so. They kept in touch but then when all this happened, I lost contact with her."

"We can work on that." Brennen reached for a paper. "Let me have the names."

"Sure. His sister was Jacqueline. My name is Irish, but they wanted something close to hers. His brother? He was Joseph, but I didn't know him well. I don't remember seeing him since before Aunt Jackie moved west. Mom said that Dad and he had words and he refused to apologize for what he said. They would never tell me what it was. He disappeared a couple of years before this happened."

"Okay. Do you know birthdates?" Brennen scribbled down the information and then was on his feet, heading for Branigan, who rose and took the paper from him, a few quiet words between them.

# Chapter 23

Jaxcy wandered the apartment the next morning, Kerry keeping pace with her. Brennen was in his office downstairs, she knew, but she refused to disturb him. She had checked the phone that he had insisted she carry. She was receiving calls from an unknown number. When she checked the voice mail, the viciousness of the messages had her dropping the phone and cowering away from it.

Heading for the door, she hesitated, jumping as a knock came to it. She peeked out, then pulled the door open.

"Branigan? Aren't you supposed to be at work?"

He simply grinned. "Not today. Today, I am working to solve your and Brennen's adventure. Would you come downstairs with me? We have some things we need to ask you about."

"And who would we be?" She slipped Kerry's leash on and then closed and locked the door. "I forgot. I should leave a note for Brennen."

"No problem. Simply send him a text."

"A text? And how would I do that?" Jaxcy was puzzled.

"On your phone." Branigan frowned as she paled. "Jaxcy? Where's your phone?"

"I left it in the apartment. I didn't tell Brennen. I have been getting calls and messages from someone. I don't know who it is. They are horrible."

Branigan reached for her keys. "Where is it?"

"On the kitchen table." She stood, arms wrapped around herself until he returned, locking the door behind him.

"We'll look into that. Dallas will need to know. Did you recognize the voice?"

Jaxcy shook her head. "No, I didn't. But then, I'm not used to talking to people over the phone. Doesn't that change the sound of the voice?"

"It can. Dallas will have the lab techs take a look at it for you. They'll retrieve the messages, analyze what they can, and then hand it off to him."

"It sounds complicated." She paused just inside the conference room door. "Branigan, what would you do, if you were me?"

"Hunt like crazy to find out if my parents were alive. Find my aunt and talk to her. See where my uncle was. Think about the trust fund and what I really wanted to do with it." He seated her, then drew up a chair beside her, his eyes on the door as Brennen entered, heading to sit beside Jaxcy.

"Jaxcy? Are you okay, Princess?" Brennen's voice soothed her fears.

"I am not sure." She pointed to the phone Branigan had laid on the table. "He's taking that. I have had calls and messages that Dallas needs to know about."

"Have you? I thought you might have. It's what they do. Threatened both of us, am I correct?"

She nodded, unwilling to put that into words. "Branigan said he needed to talk to me, but he's just sitting there, not saying anything. So, does he really need to or not?"

Branigan grinned at her, even as Brennen laughed softly. "She's got me there. Now, we have tracked down who we think is your aunt, but we need you to tell us if she is." He handed over some photos.

Jaxcy reached for them, laying them down on the table, a hand covering her mouth. "Aunt Jackie? Oh, you look so much like pictures Dad had of his mother. Where are you?"

"She's living in BC, just like you thought. Barnabas has Brody and Buckley flying out there tonight, to speak with her, not letting her know about you until we can determine why she left."

"He is? Oh, he can't do that!"

"He can and he will. He has before, Jaxcy. And he will again if he has to. The Board is in full agreement with this."

They spoke for a while longer, Jaxcy confirming more details for them as they went along. When she was not sure, she adamantly told them that. Brennen nodded. This was the Jaxcy he was falling deeper in love with. He could see her blossoming. His only fear was that she would blossom and then move on.

Late that night, Jaxcy found him as he stood on the balcony, watching the clouds playing hide and seek with the moon and stars. She slipped under the arm he held out for her, her own around him.

"Brennen? What now?"

"Now, we wait for the fellows to come back from the west. We continue to live our lives." He hugged her tighter. "I still want to take you out for a meal. We need to do that on a regular basis. Go on dates."

"Dates? Married couples do that?"

"They do. It's part of keeping fun in our lives. So, will you go out with me tomorrow night for dinner? Your choice."

She shrugged. "I guess it's safe enough. I feel afraid, Brennen, more afraid than I have ever felt. Someone is out there, watching us, just waiting for the right time to take us. I fear that we will not survive if they do."

"We are in God's hands, Jaxcy. Never forget that. He is in control. I trust Him to protect me. If He calls me home, then I am ready to go."

"I know, Brennen, but I am still afraid." She stood for a moment. "Do you think we'll ever find out what happened to my parents?"

# Chapter 24

Early the next morning, Brennen roused, his head coming up from his pillow as he squinted around the still dark room. He could hear Kerry giving soft growls from where he was positioned on the end of the bed, facing towards the door. Rising, Brennen reached for his jeans and sweatshirt that he had discarded the night before, a quick glance at the bed showing him that Jaxcy was already up. He shook his head. She rose so early, he told that if she got up any earlier, she would meet herself going to bed. She had just shaken a finger at him as she laughed.

He pulled on his socks and then motioned for Kerry to come with him. He paced through the house, Kerry's hackles rising higher and higher as they both did so. Brennen paused at his office, a frown on his face, seeing a low light, and hearing voices. Kerry was away before he could stop him, a bark sounding loudly through the room, even as Jaxcy's scream pierced the air.

Brennen was through the door, heading towards the man who stood over Kerry, who lay at his feet, blood coming from a slash on his side. Jaxcy was restrained from heading for Kerry by a second man, who had his arms tight around her, trapping hers to her side. He didn't see the third man standing just out of sight inside the room. He heard Jaxcy's scream once more before a violent blow sent him to the floor, where he lay still, sprawled facedown. He could vaguely hear Jaxcy's fear-filled voice begging them not to hurt him.

Yanked to his feet and shoved towards the balcony door, Brennen's hand rested on the back of his head, his senses still spinning. He couldn't tell if Jaxcy was with him or not, but he thought he could hear her protests that he couldn't climb down from the balcony. Shoved outside, he stood for a moment, a hand resting on the railing, before a gun poked him relentlessly in the back, and he was forced to climb over the railing to the rope ladder and then down it, one of the men heading down it before him.

Jaxcy scrambled down the ladder, fear on her face as she landed on her feet and then ran to wrap her arms around Brennen, her support helping him to stand. His arm was around her as he squinted at the men around them before they were pointed towards the woods and then through them, towards a delivery van that stood waiting, a fourth man watching closely.

Brennen stumbled inside, dropping to his knees from the hard, sudden push that sent him into the van. Jaxcy landed beside him, falling to her side, a cry of outrage and pain coming from her. The door was slammed shut and Jaxcy heard the lock clicking into place. She was on her knees, reaching for Brennen, moving them to lean again a van side, trying desperately to brace them, unable to do so as the van sped through the forest, the ruts and bumps shaking her hold on Brennen, and banging them against the metal.

"Jaxcy?" Brennen finally found his voice. "Did they hurt you?"

"No! But they did you! Brennen, your head."

Brennen shook off her hands, instead wrapping her tight to him even as he shifted them towards a corner of the van, bracing them better against the movement.

"It's okay. What happened? Where did they come from?"

"I don't know. I was up and in the kitchen, making my tea, when I heard a sound behind me. One of them slapped a hand across my mouth and then pulled me into the office. That's when I heard Kerry growling and then you coming towards me." She tucked herself tighter to him. "They came up that ladder and broke into the office through the door. They were waiting for you. If you hadn't come, they were ready to go find you." She sniffled, trying to control her tears. "Kerry!"

"I know, Princess. I know. Bradon was to head our way this morning. If we don't answer, he'll come in and look for us. He knows I would have sent a text to him if we weren't planning on meeting him. He'll look after Kerry for you."

"I know. I just don't like him laying there, hurt."

"Did they say anything?"

"No, not a word, other than they wanted you." She thought for a moment. "No, nothing more than that. Why? What would they want?"

"That's what we need to figure out." Brennen squinted towards the back of the van, feeling the vehicle slowing down and stopping. "We've stopped.

If you get a chance, run. Don't worry about me. I'll follow as best I can."

"We can't, Brennen. I won't leave you."

Brennen shook his head, his hand resting on her cheek. "Please, Princess? For me? I need you to run as fast and as far as you can, finding somewhere to hide if the opportunity presents itself." He dropped a kiss on her lips. "Please, Princess?"

Jaxcy finally nodded. "Only if you do too. I can't go on without you, Brennen."

Prevented from responding as the van door abruptly opened, Brennen raised an arm to block the strong light that blinded him. At the command to come out, he rose, Jaxcy's hand in his, and walked towards the light, a hand running along the side of the van to help him keep his balance. He was hauled from the van, landing on his knees, hearing Jaxcy's protests as pain shot through him, and his head spun from the earlier blow. How long they had been in the van, he had no idea, but he could see the faint pink on the eastern horizon.

Jaxcy twisted her body and broke free from the hold the man had on her, running to Brennen and dropping to her knees, her arms around him as his body bent forward, a hand flat on the ground bracing him to stay upright. His face contorted with pain, even as the other hand rested on the back of his head.

"Leave him alone! You've hurt him enough!" Jaxcy's cries broke through the quiet of the early morning, startling the birds and insects into flight and into quiet. Tears sparkled on her cheeks, tears that she didn't know she was shedding.

Pulled upright and away from Brennen, she watched as he was roughly hauled to his feet and pushed down a path. She continued to struggle to get away, to get to him, afraid that they would be separated. Her desperate prayer for help and safety rose, even as a damp cloth was slapped around her face. Her struggles became weaker and weaker until they ceased as her body went limp. The man holding her shook his head before he slung her over his shoulder, gruff words shared with the man who had stayed with him. They headed off towards the path, to follow the steps that Brennen and his captor had taken. The van drove slowly away, the man heading out for his normal day of deliveries.

Stillness reigned in the early morning air until the critters, birds, and insects cautiously peeked out and then began their normal daily routine. It was as if there had been no disturbance.

# Chapter 25

A frown on his face, Bradon knocked again at Brennen's door before he glanced at his watch. It was thirty minutes later than he had planned to be there, but a call from Barnabas had delayed him. He pulled out his phone, sending off a text message to Brennen and then waiting, scrolling through his own messages to see if Brennen had sent him one. None.

This is strange, he thought, before his face tightened. This was not Brennen, not to respond to a message or not to send one of his own. Lord, he prayed, I have no idea what is going on, but You do. I fear for them. Protect them. He hadn't seen them around the building, he thought, running for the stairs and then outside, searching for them.

"Brody? You're on a hunt, I can tell. Who are you looking for?" Breck stood in the building doorway.

"Brennen and Jaxcy. I don't see them anywhere. Nor Kerry. We were to meet over thirty minutes ago. I got delayed but when I knock at their door, there is no answer. And I don't hear Kerry barking."

Breck stared at him for a moment before he had turned, running for the stairs, a dark look on his face.

"And no word from him?"

"Not a one. And that's not him. He's one of the better ones of us to respond promptly to a text message."

"He is." Breck pounded at Brennen's door, causing Burnie to pop his head out of his own door before he approached them. "I'm going in, fellows. I don't like this."

Breck had keys to each of the apartments but never used them unless it was an absolute emergency or he had been asked to enter by one of the fellows. He had a bad feeling, he thought, his heart raised as well in prayer for his friend and his wife.

Searching the apartment, Breck finally approached the office, a cry drawn from him as he rushed towards Kerry. Bradon and Burnie were on his heels, Bradon dropping down beside Kerry.

"He's been slashed, not too deep, thanks to his heavy thick coat. But where are Brennen and Jaxcy?"

Burnie searched back through the apartment, finally approaching the office door to the balcony. He reached for the handle and then stopped.

"This door is open, fellows. He always locks it." He looked back over his shoulder. "I think we need to leave."

"We do." Bradon was on his feet, Kerry in his arms. "I'm heading in to the vet's with Kerry. Call me when you hear something."

"Take off, Bradon. Let us know how he is." Breck's hand rested on Kerry's head and he received a quick lick on his arm from the dog's tongue. "You're okay, Kerry. I just wish that you could talk and tell us what happened."

Two hours later, Barnabas, back from a meeting in town, approached the men, a frown on his face, as they gathered in the parking lot of the building.

"Breck? What is going on?" He searched the faces of the men, seeing the ladies waiting in the lobby.

"It's Brennen and Jaxcy. They are missing. Someone got to them." Breck kicked at a stray rock, an unusual sign of worry and frustration.

"How? The doors are locked at night." Barnabas was puzzled.

"That's not how." Burnie spoke up. "They used the office door from the balcony. The police officer we talked to thinks they had a ladder, like rope."

"They did? And they're gone?" Barnabas looked past the men as Dallas and Will walked towards them. "What about Kerry?"

"He was hurt. Bradon had him in to the vet's and now has him settled down in his crate in their apartment." Buckley shook his head. "Who would have thought?"

"I know, Buckley." Dallas spoke from beside him. "Who would have thought?" He searched the faces of the men. "When is the last time any of you saw them or heard from them?"

The men exchanged glances and shrugged.

"I guess it was likely around supper time?" Baird had a question in his voice. "Berneen had been up to see Jaxcy about going out to lunch next week. She said they seemed fine, no problems that she was aware of."

"I had a text from Brennen about seven." Bradon spoke up. "We were to meet around nine this morning. I was running late and headed there about thirty minutes later than planned."

"So, it has been what twelve to fourteen hours?" Dallas jotted notes into his ever-present notepad. "No one heard or saw anything?"

"Not a thing. Brennen's office balcony is hidden to a certain degree from the security cameras." Breck shook his head. "We thought we had it all covered."

"These people are desperate, Breck. They would have found a way." Dallas turned to study the building. "Can we go inside? It's going to take a while for you all to be spoken with. The ladies as well." Dallas watched as Doc headed their way. "Doc?"

"Any word?"

"Not a one. Did you see them this morning?" Dallas spoke up, his eyes on Will as Will studied the other man.

"No, and that's not like Brennen. He was to call early this morning. Anna said he wanted to talk to me about something to do with an illustration for a book he was working on."

# Chapter 26

Barnabas paced his office later that afternoon, his hands clasped behind his back, praying for his friends. *This is what, the ninth one, Lord? Do we have to go through all of us? How do we keep going on? This is draining all of us. It has gone on for so long. Please, Lord, bring Brennen and Jaxcy back home. And soon. And well.* Then, he sighed. *It's Your will, Lord, not ours.*

He turned as Amy, his secretary, knocked at his door.

"Yes, Amy?"

"Barnabas, I have a call from someone. He says he works for Abe and Emma. His name is Nathaniel?"

"Nathaniel? That's strange. It's usually Abe or Emma that call. Thank you, Amy." Barnabas dropped into his chair, his head bowing for a moment. He knew Abe and Emma had been searching for Jaxcy's parents, hoping to have good news. *Lord, we could use some good news.*

"Nathaniel? How are you? And Elizabeth? That's good. Yes, we do need to get our people together. Soon, I hope. But you had called?"

"I did. Abe asked me to. He's in a meeting right now with the rest of our team and Emma and Jace. We found them, Barnabas."

Barnabas stared at the wall in front of him, not seeing the enlarged photograph of an angry Lake Erie. He wasn't quite sure he had heard Nathaniel correctly.

"Barnabas? Are you there?"

"I am, Nathaniel. I'm sorry. I wasn't quite sure that I had heard you correctly." Barnabas breathed a sigh of relief.

"You did, Barnabas. We had someone in that country track them down. He's been able to move them into hiding. We're heading there shortly." Nathaniel paused, before he continued. "I tried to contact Brennen. I couldn't get any response."

Barnabas shook his head and then spoke. "No, they've disappeared. Sometime overnight, we think. We're not sure. They were taken from the apartment."

"Oh, no! This is not good. Listen, I have to run." Nathaniel could hear his name being called by Abe. "We're off, Barnabas. We'll be in prayer for those two. Abe will be in touch once we're back."

"Keep me updated as you can. We will pray here. I just hope Jaxcy and Brennen are home soon."

Barnabas set the receiver back down, before he buried his face into his hands, shudders running through him at his deep emotions. This was almost too much, Lord. To hear that her parents have been found, in another country. He raised his head, his fist resting against his chin, as he stared once more at the photo, unsure of how to approach the men, or even if he should. He looked up at the tap on his door and beckoned Breck in, asking him to close the door as he entered.

Breck sank into the chair in front of the desk, weary beyond what he had thought possible. They had searched. The police had searched. There were no signs of them. Bradon had taken Kade, his dog, out and Kade had alerted to a trail, that ended at a road. The crime scene techs were working that scene as well as the apartment and below the balcony. Dallas had privately told him that there was not a lot of evidence. It was like the couple had vanished into thin air.

"Breck? Any word?"

"Not a one. There is little evidence from what Dallas has said. We didn't think there would be. Kerry is on his feet, stressed beyond what Bradon has seen in a dog."

"I can imagine. He was there when Jaxcy disappeared. Those two share a bond that I have not seen before."

"They do. All we can do is pray. The fellows and the ladies are in the conference room. Hailey and Hollie have the twins. They said that was their job right now. Darbie is around somewhere. I'm just not sure what he is up to." Breck studied his lifelong friend. "Something has happened."

"There has been a development. I need to let you in on it, but we need to keep it between us for now. If Jaxcy was here, I would go to her and talk to her. Nathaniel called."

"Nathaniel? As in Abe's Nathaniel?"

"That one. He said the team is heading out. They found Jaxcy's parents."

Breck stilled as he stared at Barnabas. "What did you say?"

"I said, they found her parents. They're heading out to bring them home." Barnabas slumped back in his chair. "To tell you the truth? I thought that they were dead and buried somewhere or dumped into the ocean."

"That's what I thought. Brennen told me that he and Jaxcy had come to the conclusion that her parents were dead and had been for years. Now, what do we do?" Breck leaned forward, reaching for the pad of paper and pen on the corner of the desk.

"The apartment next to Brennen? Have the cleaners go through it. Make sure it's ready for us. Once we know more and when Abe will bring them here, I'll have you stock it with supplies. Talk to Anna and Doc. Prepare them. Nathaniel didn't say where Jaxcy's parents were, what country, so I have no idea what to expect."

"None of us do." Breck sighed as his phone rang. "Dallas? Any word?" He shook his head at the question on Barnabas' face. "Nothing? That's what we had thought. No, I don't know what to think. They wouldn't leave like that. Jaxcy would not leave Kerry hurt unless she was forced away. I agree. We'll spread out later and look. That property? I see. Sure, we'll keep in touch."

Barnabas had been listening closely. "No word?" His question was out almost before Breck had finished his call.

"Not a word. Not a sign. There is just nothing there."

# Chapter 27

A day later, Barnabas reached for his phone, setting down the towel that he had dried his hands on. It was late evening and he had just managed to prepare his dinner. He sighed as he stared down at his plate, thinking it would be another night that he didn't eat.

"Carey." He struggled for a moment to hear before the sound clarified. "Abe? That's you?"

"It is, Barnabas. This is a quick call. We're on our way to the plane and heading home. We have the packages that Nathaniel talked about. Give us about twenty-four hours and we'll be setting down near you." The call dropped before Barnabas could ask anything more.

His head dropping, he breathed a sigh of relief, before he reached for his plate and headed for his office. He didn't often eat in there, but this was one time he would. Barnabas sat, his head bowing as he prayed, thanking God for the fact that Jaxcy's parents were finally on their way home. He had gotten the sense that it was still dangerous for Abe and his men and would be until they were in the air and then home. He didn't think he could do what they did.

His prayer finished, Barnabas reached for his fork, eating quickly and absentmindedly as he jotted notes. He wiped his mouth on his napkin and then reached for his phone, pausing to pray once more, to plead for Brennen and Jaxcy to come home and soon.

"Breck? Are you at home?"

"I am. Do you need me?"

"I do. We need to meet. I have news." Barnabas heard the silence of the phone before Breck blew out a breath.

"Brennen?"

"No. Jaxcy's parents. Abe got a message to me. We need to make some plans." Barnabas could hear Breck's apartment door slam and then shortly his own apartment door opening and closing.

"In the office, Breck. The coffee's fresh."

"Thanks. Do you need a refill?"

"No, I'm fine for now." Barnabas was on his feet, heading for a filing cabinet, pulling out paperwork. "We'll need to talk to Doc and Anna. The cleaners have been through?"

"Just today. They said everything was good. No issues with anything." Breck sank into a chair, his mug of coffee landing on a coaster on the desk. "Where do we start?"

"We have. With the apartment. As to food? That is a big question. I would start simple, with the basics. Fresh fruit, vegetables, fish, chicken."

"Right. We have no idea where they have been?" Breck sighed as Barnabas shook his head. "Maybe Abe will call again and that will let us know what to do."

"He might. Doc will need to see them. Who do we have that we can bring in on the quiet to assess them psychologically?"

"I would say go out of town. Maybe Doug's Darcie?"

"Good idea. I know she would help. Call them in the morning. Now, we need to talk to the fellows. Set up a conference in the morning. Ladies included." Barnabas watched as Breck sent out a text, setting up the urgent conference, and smiled at how quickly the phone chimed in text messages.

"They never let us down." Breck smiled at Buckley's comment. "Buckley wants to know if we need to up the urgency on the prayer chain.'

"That won't hurt. Just put it out as an added unspoken request for Brennen and Jaxcy." Barnabas rose, then stood, staring down at the paperwork he had pulled. "We have no idea where or why."

"I suspect it was one of his siblings, Barnabas."

"I agree. Emma has been working that for us?"

"She has. Burnie said he had found some interesting information that he needed to share with us concerning them. I will ask him about it tomorrow."

The following morning, Barnabas stared around the chapel, seeing each one of the men and the ladies there. Doc and Anna and Amy were there. He had asked Andy to be present, thinking that if Abe landed in his own town, he would send Andy that way.

"Fellows. Ladies. We have news." Barnabas' voice broke through the chatter and created silence. "No, we have not found Brennen or Jaxcy. Abe has called. He is on his way home from somewhere with Jaxcy's parents."

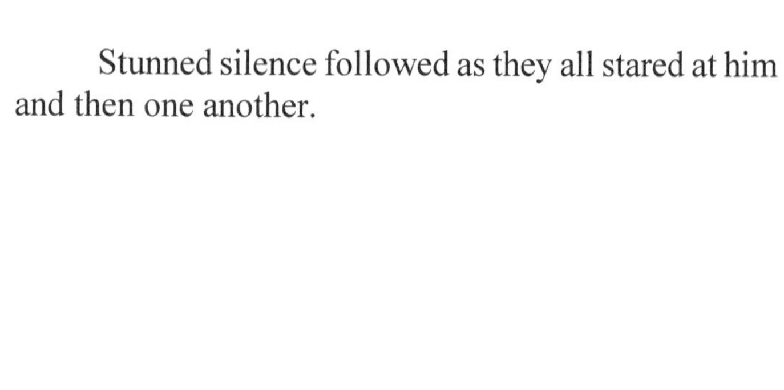

Stunned silence followed as they all stared at him and then one another.

Chapter 28

Early the next evening, Barnabas walked towards the Foundation plane, watching as Doc, Brady, and Breck emerged, an older couple with them. Abe had been in touch early that morning, requesting that Barnabas send his plane to meet them. He felt that they had been followed and he didn't feel comfortable heading to them. Barnabas had agreed, set up a meeting at a remote airport. All the men and the ladies had volunteered to go. He had thanked them, picked the three men, and sent them on their way.

Breck moved quickly towards him, pointing to the vehicles. "We just made it off the runway when vehicles appeared. Someone has been watching us too closely, Barnabas. Let's get them out of sight in the Building."

"Agreed. Have they said much?" Barnabas watched as Brady and Doc headed the couple for the van.

"No, not a lot. Other than a thank you, and how did we know?" Breck shook his head. "They're not in great shape at the moment. He did mention that things had gotten rougher the last couple of months."

"About the time this started with Brennen and Jaxcy. Did you tell them about Jaxcy?"

"No, I thought that it would be best coming from you. They have not asked how or why we found them.

Abe didn't give much information, we were that concerned about getting them transferred and then getting back in the air."

"I understand. Head off home, Breck. I'll follow when Andy is ready."

Andy approached him shortly. "Barnabas? Did Breck tell you?"

"He did." Barnabas reached for the thumb drive Andy was holding out. "Captured some pictures, did you?"

"I did. I can't guarantee how clear, but we did our best." He shook his head. "To think they have been alive and Jaxcy thought they were dead."

"I know. It's going to be tough for each of them, isn't it? I just wish we had Jaxcy here."

"I know. It's going to go hard. Any idea on who is behind it?"

Barnabas shook his own head. "Just speculation at the present."

"I would say her aunt."

"Why?" Barnabas parked in his assigned slot and then shifted to stare at Andy.

"I don't know. It would just make awful sense, now wouldn't it? But then again, it could be her uncle. Did her mother have any family?"

"That we can't determine. For some reason, it's too hidden. Emma and Jace are working their magic as is Kataleen with her family tree program. She was finding some interesting items, she tells me."

Andy grinned as he shut the SUV door. "She will do her best. She finds things I couldn't imagine finding. By the way, Abe said Darcie is willing to come to talk with Jaxcy's parents."

"That's good to know. Thanks, Andy. Have a good night."

Andy waved as he walked away, Barnabas standing for a moment in the quiet of the twilight, his face tilted to the sky, his eyes closed as he breathed a prayer of thankfulness but also of intercession, begging for his friend and his wife to come home and soon.

Breck watched him from nearby, waiting until Barnabas turned towards him.

"Did you get them settled?"

"As well as we could. Her father said it is such a contrast. They basically lived in a rundown shack that had no amenities and had holes in the roof and walls. I would like to get my hands on whoever it was."

"You and me both." Barnabas held the lobby door. "I'm heading up to meet them. Do I need to know anything in particular?"

Breck gave a shake of his head. "Not really. They're quiet, as could be expected. They are in shock at being free after all these years. I would say to give them a few days to get accustomed to that, then have Dallas meet with them. Buckley has already been around and introduced himself, planning on meeting with them in the morning. Doc has assessed them quickly, he said, but he would like to do more, run bloodwork, and whatnot, as he puts it." Breck suddenly grinned. "Jaxcy is almost the image of her mother. Both are petite ladies."

"That's good to know. Have a good night, Breck. Thanks again." Barnabas headed for the stairs to climb to the second floor, Breck watching as he walked away.

# Chapter 29

The next morning, Barnabas watched as Jaxcy's parents walked towards him across the lobby, fear and apprehension on their faces. He sighed. This is not how it was to be, he thought. Lord, this time, You need to work through this. It will take years for them to become accustomed to being free once more. What was it, eleven years or so?

"Mr. Carey?" Jaxcy's father, Jeremiah, held out his hand. "Once more, thank you. Jemma and I can't begin to tell you how grateful we are."

"It's Barnabas, please. I just wish we had known before. We would have brought you home sooner if we had known."

Jaxcy's mother simply reached up to hug him. He grinned to himself. Breck was right. Jaxcy was a lot like her petite mother.

"I just wish Jaxcy was here. Let's have a seat here in the lobby." Barnabas looked up as Fynn approached, a tray in her hand. "Here, thank you, Fynn. This is Fynn, Brady's wife."

"Brady's wife? The one he says likes to play with creepy-crawlies?" Jeremiah gave a small grin. "He talked of you last night, in part I think to help ease us into here. Between the three men, we have a good idea of who is who here."

"That's great. We just keep expanding our family. I won't stay." Fynn turned to leave, when Jemma grasped her hand.

"Please? Brady said you had connected with Jaxcy. Please? I need to know about her. We both do. It's been too long. We were told she had overdosed and died, that we had to leave the country because the police had determined we had provided the drugs to her." Jemma shared a look with Jeremiah. "We couldn't defend ourselves. We were never given a chance."

Fynn sat beside Jemma, her hand tight in the older lady's grip. "That is so wrong. And Jaxcy was told you two were dead. Did you know that?"

"Breck told us that last night. Who would be so cruel?" Jemma wiped at her eyes.

Barnabas had been watching Jeremiah and then spoke quietly to the older man. "You have an idea?"

"I do. I would like to talk to you and that Breck, today, if possible. I don't like to accuse anyone but someone is responsible for breaking up our family. Jemma and I have talked it over until there was nothing left to talk over. We could barely scrape by to make a living. It was hard, Barnabas. Almost like being in a prison. And in fact, that is what we were told we were in. I can't thank you or that Abe and his men enough."

"That's what Abe does, goes in and rescues people. We'll talk. The men are working away today, hoping to bring a swift resolution to this." Barnabas spoke quietly with Jeremiah, listening to Fynn draw out Jemma. Brady, you sell your wife short. She is doing just what needs to be done, asking the questions that need to be asked.

Jemma finally looked at him. "Do you know where our daughter is? I want to see her so much."

"I am so sorry. I don't. I wish I did." Barnabas looked at Fynn, who was watching Jemma with a compassionate look on her face. "Jemma, would you feel comfortable meeting some of the other ladies?"

"I guess." Jemma shared a look with Jeremiah before she nodded. "If that is what you wish, I can."

"No, it's not what I wish. It is what you wish and want to do. You are free here. You decide how you live your life." Barnabas watched with compassion her struggle before she nodded.

"It's hard, Barnabas. We have not had freedom in so long."

"We understand. Now, let's go find the ladies. I'm sure you'll enjoy Hagen's twins." Fynn rose, drawing Jemma to her feet, and linking an arm with Jemma.

"Twins? Oh, my!" Jemma walked away with Fynn, Fynn chattering away.

"That's not Fynn, to chatter like that."

"I didn't think it was. Now, Barnabas, tell me what you couldn't or wouldn't in front of Jemma."

Barnabas rose and pointed to a hallway. "Let's go meet with the men. Dallas, the police detective, will be out shortly. And Will Peters, our police chief, is heading our way. He stated that he wants to meet Jaxcy's parents and thank them."

"Thank us? For what? Bringing trouble to Brennen?" Jeremiah was puzzled.

"No, he wanted to thank them for raising a resourceful daughter who brings sunlight to everyone who meets her."

# Chapter 30

Brady moved across the room to where Breck stood, staring at the map they had placed there.

"Any thoughts?"

"I wonder how close they are to here. I can't see them being too far away." Breck traced a finger along the road that tracked along a portion of the Foundation grounds. "Dallas said they have gone into the house that Smithers was using. No sign of anyone there in a while, he said."

"No, that would be too obvious. But then, obvious is how things usually work out." Benen spoke from behind them. "We have had them close to us or farther away. Blair and I have been monitoring the lake. No signs of any boats out there that don't belong."

"Good thought." Burnie reached for a tack and a string, tying the string to the tack, which he then placed in the centre of the Foundation building. "If we start with a small circle, can we trace who has the land or buildings? Most of them we know and would not be involved in anything against us. At least, not willingly."

"No, they wouldn't." Breck stepped back to let Burnie work, hearing the steps behind him as the other men approached. "So, where does this leave us?"

"We tackle what's in this circle and then keep expanding." Burnie looked over his shoulder as Dallas made a sound. "Dallas?"

"You've thought of something that I'm not sure we have. We have been struggling with trying to determine properties and owners, given the workload that we're under right now." He suddenly grinned at Burnie. "Want to come join us? We have an opening in the detective pool."

Burnie gave him a horrified look. "No, thank you very much. I'll stick to writing the mysteries. I couldn't solve them in real life."

"But, Burnie, that is exactly what we are doing." Brandon grinned at him. "Or did you think this didn't count that way?"

Burnie glared at him for a moment before he grinned. "I know. That's not how I meant to say it."

"We know, Burnie. You're better at writing than at speaking at times." Brendon ducked the pretend blow that Burnie sent his way.

Jeremiah stood beside Barnabas, a frown on his face as he listened to the men joking, not quite sure how life worked anymore.

"It's okay, Jeremiah. They're just letting off their worry and frustration. They are all good friends. They come from every province and territory, are all orphans for some reason or another. They care deeply about one another. I am sure that you are aware we've been solving the mysteries and adventures that the others have been involved in."

"The men mentioned it last night." Jeremiah gazed around the room, seeing the piles of paper, the computers, printers, faxes, and other equipment that he just could not name. "I really didn't understand."

"No? It's strange when we are all involved in different lines of employment and volunteer work. Brennen is a child's book illustrator and he volunteers with a baseball team for small children. They love him."

"Breck, I think it was, mentioned that last night. Jaxcy? What does she do?"

"That's the thing, Jeremiah. Here, have a seat." Barnabas waited until the older man had sat, a mug of coffee set in front of him, before he too sat and then began to talk. "Jaxcy doesn't talk a lot about what she wants to do. The house you had was taken from her. We're working on that. She had to scrimp and scrape just to get by. Coming here was a sharp contrast for her, she has said. She didn't have an opportunity to go away and go to college. She is really not sure what she wants to do. Brennen is content just to let her heal and then make her choices. She will not want for money. As a member of the Foundation family, she is provided with an income."

"She is? Thank you, son." Jeremiah's face worked as he tried to control his emotions. A second broken thank you came from him even as he reached a handkerchief to his face to wipe away his tears. He jumped as he felt a dog stand up at his knee and lick at his face.

"This is Kerry." Barnabas' hand rested on Kerry's head. "He belongs to Jaxcy. He was hurt the night that they disappeared."

"Kerry, is it? She has always liked that name." The older man's hand rested on the dog's neck even as he studied him. "Thank you, then, Kerry, for trying to protect our girl."

The men had found their seats as Barnabas and Jeremiah were speaking, breaking into groups of twos to pray before they straightened their chairs around, their gaze on Barnabas.

# Chapter 31

The men had tossed ideas around, listened closely as one another spoke, before Dallas rose, heading to renew his mug of coffee, a frown on his face. His mug hit the table with a bang, before he was back at a computer, working through his various passwords to access a secure site. He typed rapidly, watching the monitor as screens flicked over one by one. Will sat beside him, quiet conversation between them before Dallas sat back, pointing to a name.

"That one. That's the one that I think we missed. How did we do that?"

Will nodded. "I agree." He sighed. "Who was working on that portion?"

Dallas shot him a look and then sighed. "Are you thinking they overlooked this on purpose?"

"I do." Will rose. "I know who it is. You don't need to say anything. I'm heading in to talk to Ralph. He'll pull the detective in."

Dallas watched him walk away, seeing Brendon slip into the chair that Will had just vacated. His fingers moved to close the program.

"Dallas?"

"Yeah, Brendon. We have someone who wasn't doing what they were supposed to be doing. Will's heading in to talk to Ralph."

"That doesn't sound good." Brendon studied Jeremiah, seeing the fatigue that was starting to him down. "We need to get Jeremiah out of here. He's weary."

Dallas turned to watch him. "He is. And I need to be on my way. Thanks for the input. You fellows always have insight into a situation that is different from ours."

"That's because we aren't police officers. And coming from our varied backgrounds, it is a given that we see things differently." Brendon rose as Dallas did. "I just wish I knew where they were. We need to get them home."

"That we do. We're working on it, Brendon. Keep on doing what you fellows are. Send me any information that you can. Emma and Jace are doing that. I just don't get where she finds what she does." Dallas shook his head at that even as he turned to walk away.

Two hours later, Brandon rose abruptly and headed for the map, his finger tracing outside the circle that Burnie had drawn before he nodded. His gaze dropped to the paper that he held. A small cry rose from him, causing the others in the room to turn and stare at him.

"Brandon? Care to share with us?" Brody rose, to stand beside him, staring at the area that Brandon still had his finger planted on. "There? Why?"

Brandon shook the papers in the air. "Because of this. Emma sent over some addresses. This is one that we would never have looked at. It's buried in numbered companies." Brandon turned to the room, searching for Jeremiah, and breathing a sigh of relief that he wasn't there. "It's connected to Jaxcy's aunt and uncle."

"The two of them? I thought there was a split in the family." Benen moved towards the map. "There? Of course. So close, but so far. When do we head over there?"

Barnabas had entered as they were speaking. "First, let's get organized. Brandon, talk to us. Then, we pray. Then, we make plans."

Late that night, the black SUV crept slowly down a side road before it pulled into a laneway and stopped, the lights going off. Three men emerged and headed quickly and silently down the laneway, pausing frequently to listen. The agreement had been to head into the building and search it, being back out before daylight fell.

Their steps paused as they heard hesitant, staggering footsteps heading their way, looks exchanged between them before they faded into the overhanging limbs. A slight cry came from one before the three were running towards the man heading their way, a burden in his arms. They moved the man quickly towards the SUV, one of them taking his burden from him, the other two swinging his arms over their shoulders to support him. They shoved him onto a seat, placing his burden near him, and climbed in, the SUV disappearing quickly from sight down the road.

The driver gave a quick glance behind him, a questioning look on his face, before he nodded at the explanation given him. He drove towards the back building entrance of the Foundation building, the large overhead door to the loading dock raising to allow him entry, closing silently behind him.

Doc and Brady stood beside the two stretchers pulled up near the vehicle, watching closely as the doors swung open and the men emerged, pulling Brennen out and leading him to a stretcher, countering his attempts to get back to the vehicle. Doc's hands were there as Jaxcy was pulled from the vehicle, her body limp and unresponsive as she was carried carefully to the other stretcher and laid there, a blanket pulled up over her to try and counter the shivers that shuddered through her body.

Barnabas stood watching, thankful that his friends were back, before he looked up at Breck.

"Breck?"

"We found them walking towards us, Barnabas. I don't know how. It was as if Brennen was determined to walk all the way back here."

"And he would have. Go with them. We'll meet shortly." Barnabas rubbed at his face. "It's late. The five of us will meet, the rest of us in the morning." He walked towards the building infirmary. "I'll speak with her parents in the morning, once we know more. I don't like her looks."

"No, she's struggling to breathe. Brennen is worn out. He looks as if he's been beaten again. She's been beaten too. Who does this?" Breck was worried and frustrated.

"We'll find then, Breck. We'll find them. We need to keep these two safe, and just how we do that, I'm not sure anymore."

———

# Chapter 32

Standing back from the door, Jeremiah pointed to the kitchen of the apartment that they were using. Barnabas rested a hand on his shoulder for a moment before he headed to the kitchen, a greeting for Jemma sounding from him. Buckley followed, a prayer raising in his heart, knowing that what they had to say would bring happiness but also worry.

Jemma turned from the counter, reaching to return Barnabas' hug. She had never liked to hug in the past, at least hug those who were not her family. She had discovered that she now liked that contact with people, finding it was helping her to heal. The ladies of the building had started that with her, hugging her every time that they met her. They were a blessing, she thought.

Buckley hugged her as well before reaching for the coffee pot and pouring coffee for them all, just grinning at her protest.

"It's okay, Jemma. It's what we do, serve one another. We don't even think about it anymore."

Jeremiah finally spoke, his eyes on Jemma as he did so. "You two boys are here early this morning. As much as we have come to enjoy your company, you must have a reason."

Buckley spoke up. "We do, Jeremiah. First, may I pray with you two?"

Jemma nodded, having become accustomed to Buckley's way of dealing with life and stress. "Prayer would be good. I have been awake all night, burdened for our girl and her man."

Barnabas sipped at his mug of coffee when Buckley finished, trying to organize his thoughts, something unusual for him.

"Barnabas? You have word?" Jeremiah's words were hesitant once more, fear evident in them.

"We do, Jeremiah. Jemma. Last night, Breck took Benen, Burnie, and Branigan. They headed out just about dark, to a place that Brandon had discovered. The rest of us waited in the chapel, bathing their trek in prayer. I won't go into the details of how or where. That has been given to Dallas, and he is dealing with it. Breck, Benen, and Branigan headed down an overgrown laneway. Partway down it, they heard a noise and drew off to the side. They recognized the man heading their way, met him, and brought him home."

"Brennen!" Jemma's quiet voice held confidence that she was right. "He's home. Jaxcy?"

Barnabas shared a look with Buckley, seeing the worry in his friend's eyes. "We have her. She's home, Jemma. Jeremiah." He struggled to control his own emotions as the older couple simply held each other and wept, the emotions overcoming them.

When he could finally speak, Jeremiah had to clear his throat frequently. "Take us to her. I assume that she is in a hospital."

"No, she's here. We have an infirmary set up on the first floor. Doc is with her. So is Anna. Cadee is training as a nurse and is there." Barnabas' hand on his arm kept Jeremiah in his chair. "She is sick, Jeremiah. Pneumonia, Doc tells me. She has also been beaten as has Brennen. That worries Doc. We don't know if there are any residual effects from that."

"Please, Barnabas? Take us to her?" Jemma was on her feet, her hands reaching for the mugs, to rinse them out, rinsing out the coffee pot, and emptying the grounds into the garbage before any of the men could stop her.

Barnabas hesitated at the infirmary door, his eyes on the couple. "Doc is here. He'll let you stay for a while, but only for a while. He's trying to find a treatment for her. He'll need to get a medical history from you. When she had her broken jaw, Brennen refused some treatment for her, just because he didn't know her history."

"I see." Jeremiah's arm tightened around Jemma. "Unless she has developed something since we last saw her, then the answer would be that she has no history."

Jeremiah and Jemma entered the room hesitantly, their eyes on Doc before they moved forward, to stand at their daughter's bedside. Jemma's hand shook as she reached to touch her daughter's face and hair in ever so many years.

Doc and Cadee stood back, watching, Doc's eyes concerned that this might be too much for them. He had assessed the couple completely the day before, concerned that Jeremiah had developed what he was sure was heart disease. This was not good, he thought, the stress that having Jaxcy back but sick would bring.

Jeremiah kept an arm around his wife, his heart breaking for her and for their daughter, and the young man who was now part of their family, one that they still needed to meet. His hand rested on his daughter's, feeling the fever wracking her body. His eyes lifted to the monitors and then to the IV line running to her other hand. He traced her face, seeing it in the young girl he had lifted to his shoulders so many times as she had asked him to, seeing the young teen he had helped with her homework.

As he stood there, Jeremiah grew angry as he saw the young lady that he needed to learn to know once more, anger burning in his heart at the years taken from him, before he repented and asked for forgiveness. Forgiveness for his anger but forgiveness for whoever it was. He had a suspicion as to who it was. It had become clearer overnight as he too had spent the night in intercessory prayer for his daughter and all those involved. He had stood on the balcony overlooking the parking lot, watching the men run for the vehicle and then drive away. He had still been standing there, the lights off in the apartment behind him, as it had returned and then driven out of sight around the building. He had prayed then, that his daughter had come home, as well as her groom.

It had shaken both of them, he knew, to find out that Jaxcy had lived as she had, had married in such a manner, but they knew her character of the past. They knew that she would have stepped in as she had, without a thought for her own safety. So much had been taken from them, so many years that they would never get back. His eyes were raised as he heard footsteps, footsteps that sounded unsteady, before a young man stopped on the other side of the bed, his hand reaching to cup Jaxcy's face before he bent to kiss her, his cheek resting against hers.

_Chapter 33_

Jemma stood for a moment before she was around the bed, a mother's arms encircling a hurting young man, a young man who could not even remember his own mother's arms. Her soft prayer reached to him, and he began to weep, sobs rising within as her arms tightened, and then Jeremiah was there, beside them. His arms encircled his wife and son-in-law even as his prayer was raised. Doc and Cadee stepped from the room, Cadee opening weeping as Benen found her. Doc wiped at his eyes, before he raised them, shaking his head.

"It's just on much, boys." He looked around at the group gathered, each man in the building present, as were the ladies, the twins, and Darbie. Amy was there as well. He saw Bruce and Elizabeth Carey headed their way and nodded. Barnabas needed his parents, given the high emotions that all of them were dealing with.

Jeremiah finally stood back, his arm around his wife, as he studied the tall young man who stood in front of them. A hurting young man, he decided, and hurting in more ways than just physical. How he reached him in the hurt, he had no idea, but God did. He prayed for him, and then for Jemma and himself, and then for his daughter.

"You must be Brennen." Jemma reached to hug him again, feeling him clinging just a moment longer than she had expected.

"I am." Brennen was confused for a moment before his brow cleared. "Jaxcy's parents? But how?"

"We are. I'm Jemma and that's Jeremiah. A young man named Abe swept in and rescued us from where we had been taken all those years ago. We had no way of getting away or coming home. We were on an island miles from here."

"Abe did? That's wonderful. Emma must have found out where you were." Brennen's body sagged for a moment and he was grateful to sink down in the chair that Jeremiah pushed forward. "I'm sorry."

"Sorry for what?" Jeremiah rested his hand on Brennen's shoulder.

"I'm sorry that you lost all those years with Jaxcy. I'm sorry that you were treated like you were. I'm sorry that Jaxcy can't meet you again. I'm sorry that she's sick and been hurt. I'm sorry that I couldn't protect her any better than I did." He looked up at them, a lost little boy look on his face that endeared him deeply to Jemma. They had learned his story from Barnabas the day before. "But I am not sorry that Jaxcy is my love. I love her deeply, more than I ever thought I could love someone. She is a wonderful, compassionate lady. Jaxcy has had it rough but she has not let it destroy her."

"Thank you, Brennen." Jemma's voice died away as she dropped a kiss on the top of his head. "Welcome to the family. But I understand that all your friends are working hard to solve your adventure as they call it. The ladies have taken me to their hearts, and I love that. I have craved for female companionship that I would just relax and enjoy."

Brennen's gaze went back to his bride, his heart hurting that she was suffering to breathe. He wanted a piece of each of the men who had held them captive, making her slave for them, holding him away from her and against a wall as he watched her struggle to cope the last couple of days, the fever slowing her steps and fogging her mind. He knew that she had wanted to quit, but kept on going, just because of the threats levelled towards him. He had tried to intervene, told them that he would do the cooking and cleaning that they insisted she do, but blows to his face and body had stopped him.

He rose, a hand on her face, a kiss on her lips, as Doc approached, a hand out to help him from the room. Jemma and Jeremiah followed, a long last look at their daughter, before confusion in the hallway took their attention. They watched, horrified, as Brennen's legs gave way and he collapsed, only the hands of his friends keeping him from landing hard on the hardwood floor.

Doc pointed to the second infirmary room.

"In there. I thought that this would happen." He looked around, spying Dallas. "Find them, Dallas. Find the monsters who hurt these two. This building family? It's had enough. Stop this insanity." He was behind the closed door, Anna and Cadee with him, Brady on his heels.

———

Late the next afternoon, Brennen stood once more beside Jaxcy's bed, his eyes worried, as he listened to Doc. Jaxcy was not responding how he wanted her to. It might mean that she needed to be in the hospital and that Brennen was reluctant to do. But, he thought, if she had to be, he would do that.

"What can we do for her here, Doc? That we haven't already done?"

"Not much else, but if she needs more aggressive treatment, then that's where we'll need to move her. I would rather do it sooner than later."

Brennen nodded, knowing that Doc was being brutally honest with him. "I know, Doc. I know. It's just such a risk, taking her there. She can be reached there."

"And she can here. Not as easily." Doc sighed. "I'll wait until later tonight and see where she stands."

"Thank you, Doc." Brennen didn't move as Doc walked away. He couldn't. He prayed harder, he thought, than he had prayed in his life. Please, Lord, don't let my lady die. Please? I need her. Her parents need her. The ones in the building need her. Someone is out there that she needs to reach.

Late that night, Brennen looked up from where he sat, his head bowed, the bruising on his face looking garish in the soft light. He was on his feet, his hand reaching for Jaxcy as she moved, a moan coming from her even as she coughed. Her hand reached for the oxygen mask that covered her face. Brennen's other hand stopped hers from moving it.

Jaxcy's eyes flickered open and closed even as she licked at her lips. She frowned at him.

"Brennen? What time is it?"

"Almost midnight."

"What day?"

"It's Saturday. Why?"

"Then, we have to move. They're going to take us away from here. That's what they said. The leader didn't care if I heard them. They're taking us out of the country." She was becoming agitated.

"We're safe, Princess. We're safe. We're home."

"Home? We can't be. They won't let us go."

"No, they didn't. I managed to get us away. Breck and some of the fellows met us and brought us home."

She nodded, her eyes fever bright. "Take me home, Brennen. I can't do this anymore. Take me home, please." She slept, her sleep natural for the first time in days.

Brennen stood, his eyes on her, a thought crossing his mind that he shrugged off. Did he really just walk out of there, or had they let him go for a reason? What did Jaxcy mean when she said they were to be taken out of the country?

He watched her closely, her words asking him to take her home resounding in his mind. If that was what she wanted, then he would. He would take her back to the Rock, fix up her cabin, and live there with her. He would bring in electricity, figure out the internet somehow. He could work from anywhere. He would miss his friends and the community that the building people were, but Jaxcy came first.

Jemma had entered quietly as Jaxcy was speaking. She had hesitated about moving forward, not wanting to disturb the younger couple. Her hand on Brennen's back startled him.

"She was awake?"

"She was, Jemma. She was. She's confused." Brennen's brow wrinkled for a moment.

"She never does illness well. And for her to be this sick, makes it worse." Jemma's arm was around him. "Don't rush into any decisions. She asks things in her sickness that she would never ask otherwise. She never means them."

"I think she does this time. She wants to go home."

"And this is your home. She will make it hers. You two have not had what you would even consider a regular marriage, now have you?"

Brennen shook his head, a smile crossing his face. "None of us have. You have heard the adventures that my friends have had. How do we continue?"

"By trusting God. Trusting your friends. Trusting that police detective who comes around every once in a while." Jemma paused. "He is a troubled young man, seeking for something that he hasn't found yet. He will not stay in that department much longer."

"You don't think so? Strange. That's how I feel."

Jemma nodded towards her daughter. "Don't make a decision based on her illness. If you want to keep her home down there, fix it up. Use it as a retreat. Or let someone else use it, who really needs it."

Brennen stared down at the lady that he was beginning to think of as his mother. He dropped a kiss on her cheek. "Thank you. You are a wise lady."

"I have had a lot of years just to think and pray. A forced retreat, if you will." She studied him for a moment. "Jaxcy loves you. I heard her responding to you. She doesn't do that with people who are not important to her."

Brennen nodded, his eyes on his princess. "I always dreamed of a princess, of being a prince or a knight riding in on a white horse to save her. She is my princess, Jemma."

"She is, Brennen. And you rode in to save her. Not on a white horse, but nonetheless, you saved her from a fate that her father and I can only imagine awaited her." Jemma reached to kiss her daughter, reached to hug Brennen, and walked away, leaving Brennen with his thoughts, some of which were black.

# Chapter 35

A day or so later, wrapped in a heavy blanket, her feet tucked up on the couch, Jaxcy rested tightly against Brennen, unwilling to move too far from him. Kerry was draped across her lap, he too unwilling to leave either one of them. He had licked and washed at Jaxcy's face when he saw her, not ready to leave her alone. Her arms had tightened around him, unable to let him go.

She nodded as she listened to the quiet conversation around her. Barnabas and his father, Bruce, were there. Her mother and father moved quietly around, handing out the mugs of coffee and tea that had been requested. Breck had come in, checked on her, and then quietly sat where he could watch them both.

Buckley had been around earlier, as had Fynn. Praying for them both, Buckley had asked no questions, not needing to. Fynn had been there, helped Jaxcy to shower and then change into clean clothes. Her kindness and willingness to serve had brought tears to Jaxcy's eyes and earned her a long hard hug. She had not stayed, waving at Jeremiah and Jemma as she left.

Jaxcy was not quite sure how to handle having her parents back in her life. To find out that they were still alive had been traumatic, but to actually have them in her home? That would take some getting used to.

She thought of all the tears, sorrow, rage, fear, and whatever other emotion she had been through in the past years. Lord, You need to help me. I can't do this. Not anymore. I just want to go home, but this is my home. I know Brennen would move back east, but that's not his home. I just am so confused.

Brennen's arm tightened around his princess. He knew she was at her limit but she had refused to leave him. He could understand that. Looking up as Bruce started to pray, his eyes slid closed and he felt the presence of God in the room. He always did when Bruce prayed.

No one wanted to break the silence when the prayer time had ended. Jeremiah finally spoke, his eyes on Jemma as he did so.

"Have you talked to that police detective, Brennen?"

"We have. I can share some of our story, but some of it has to be kept silent."

"That we can understand. Just tell us what you can." Barnabas sat forward, his eyes on his friend. "How did they manage to surprise you, with Kerry here?"

"That's what we're not sure of. We talked about it. Kerry was still on the bed when I woke to his growling. Jaxcy hadn't been up for long, just long enough to make her tea. She said that as she finished, she sensed someone in the room with her. A hand was over her mouth and her arms were trapped to her sides before she was carried to the office.

"I think it was at that point I woke to Kerry's growling. I don't understand why he didn't leave me. I got up dressed and starting searching for Jaxcy, hearing men's voices that I didn't recognize. I found her in the office, saw her being restrained, and then I was down. I didn't see the third man standing beside the door, waiting for me. Jaxcy managed to get to me, but I couldn't help her escape. We were forced out on the balcony and then down a rope ladder."

"We wondered at that." Barnabas spoke up. "Dallas said there wasn't much evidence."

"No, I don't think there would have been. They had us down the ladder, the ladder retrieved Jaxcy said, and then we were forced to walk to the side road near us. They had a delivery van of some kind. We were forced into it. They drove around for a while, always on rough roads, but it felt like they had been driving in circles.

"When they stopped, we were forced out. I was led away before Jaxcy was. I am not sure what happened next. Jaxcy was chloroformed, that we figured out."

"Chloroform? That's an old trick." Bruce looked up from his notes. "Did you get a good look at the van or any of the men?"

"Not really. I know the van was high enough that I could stand almost upright. That's not much help."

"A delivery van, then." Bruce nodded. "We'll see what we can do. Now, what else?" His gaze shifted to Jaxcy, a small smile creeping to his face as he noticed her nodding off. "Jaxcy, what can you tell us?"

Jaxcy blinked, bringing her attention to Bruce. "I'm not sure. I was too worried about Brennen to see much. I know there were four, but only three went with us. The three that were in the apartment. One of them headed away with Brennen first. I don't remember what happened after that until I awoke." She shivered for a moment, her fever starting to spike again. She blinked again, her eyes sore.

"Just tell us the basics, then. We can always get more information later." Bruce smiled at her.

# Chapter 36

Jaxcy had awoken during the late morning, disoriented for a moment, shivering at the chill in the room. She had reached for the blanket crumpled beside her, wrapping herself in it, before looking around through blurry eyes. Frowning, she stared at the body lying near her before she scrambled to her knees, to crawl towards it.

She pulled at the man, turning him towards her, shocked to find Brennen there. She shook him, calling his name, unable to rouse him. Sitting, a hand on his chest, she stared around, trying to make sense of what was going on. Unable to, she had reached for the blanket on the floor beside him, spreading it out to cover him, laying down beside him, her own blanket covering her. She pulled his arm around her, a hand on his wrist to keep it there, her other arm across his chest. Head on his shoulder, Jaxcy slept, unable to stay awake.

Neither one heard the door open or the heavy footsteps that approached them. The man stood, staring down at them, hatred on his face. It was their fault, he decided. Their fault that he didn't get the money coming to him that should have come. They would pay. He turned and walked away, the door clicking shut behind him and the lock snapping closed.

Brennen had awakened in the early morning, a toe shoving at his ribs doing that. He had sat up, rubbing at his head, his eyes on the man. He rose when he was told to, finding Jaxcy on her feet, her wrist tight in the grasp of another man. Jaxcy had shaken her head at him, her eyes trying to communicate with him, but his head was pounding too much to understand what she was attempting to tell him.

Jaxcy had been pulled to the kitchen, finding it in shambles, uncertain as to what was expected of her. She heard Brennen's stumbling footsteps and tried to look around the man holding her. The leader of the three stood in front of her, a black look on his face.

"You will clean this kitchen. You will cook for us. Then, you will clean the house." His words were abrupt, guttural, almost, she thought, as if he was trying to disguise his voice.

"No. I won't. I'm not your servant." A sudden blow across her face had her on the floor, tears blinding her. She could vaguely hear Brennen's shout of outrage and the struggle he put up to get to her. Hauled to her feet, shaken by the hands that held her, Jaxcy was again ordered to clean and cook. She started to refuse until her eyes found Brennen and drew in her breath.

Brennen was held to the wall in front of her, his arms twisted near his side, pain evident on his face. He could barely stand, she thought, seeing the red marks the blows to his face had left. Her own hand touched her face, finding the cut on her lip and the blood trickling from it. She shook, more from fear than anything. Lord, what have we gotten into? Protect Brennen. Set him free. She finally nodded, not looking at the man.

Working quickly, Jaxcy had cleared enough of the debris and dirty dishes to be able to prepare the men's breakfast, wanting to slap it on the table, but knowing that if she did, Brennen might pay. The men sat to eat, ordering Brennen to stay where he was and Jaxcy to move to the other side of the room. They were warned to stay exactly where they were or the other one would be hurt.

Jaxcy grew fatigued, the effects of the chloroform still evident in her body, as she finished scrubbing the kitchen and then moved to clean the rest of the house. She sighed. How could men live like this? Her mother would have had a few choice words about the state of the house. Jaxcy was blinded by tears as she worked, just missing her mother and wanting to see her. Anger at herself drove her forward until the house was clean, but not sparkling. That, Jaxcy decided, would never happen. It needed paint and new flooring for that, and she doubted that the men would be bothered doing that.

Brennen turned as the door opened to the room they had been shoved into. He waited, his eyes on Jaxcy as she stumbled through the door, the leader of the men standing staring at him, a warning on his lips to not try anything. No sooner had the door closed and the lock clicked then Brennen was across the room, catching Jaxcy as she collapsed, her head hitting his shoulders. He looked around, finding no chair, only the rough mattress shoved into a corner. He hurried that way, sitting down and just cradling her to him, a blanket wrapped around her.

Jaxcy was too tired, she thought, too tired to do anything. Too tired to talk to Brennen. Too tired to sleep. She just stayed in his arms, feeling the strength and caring and love in them.

"Jaxcy? Are you okay?" Brennen kept his voice low.

"I think so. Just overly tired." She tilted her head back. "And you? Did they hurt you this morning?"

"Not really. They did you." His finger gently touched her face and lip. "I wanted to hurt them, Jaxcy, for hurting you."

"I know, love. I know. We have to stay strong. We have to find a way out, only I'm not so sure that we can." She grew quiet, finally sleeping.

Brennen didn't stir that night, his head going down on hers as he too slept. He had tried to stay awake, tried to plan what to do, but the effects of the blow to his head and the beating he had taken that morning were too much. His body needed to recover, and sleep was part of how it would.

## *Chapter 37*

The same pattern happened day after day. Jaxcy still refused the initial request to clean and cook, until she saw the abuse that Brennen took. They both realized that it was happening to force her to work for the men. She stared at them in distaste, wishing she could somehow escape but knowing that was not a possibility. She grew desperate as the days went by.

Brennen searched the room they were in, trying to find a way out, but unable to. It was an older home, with older wooden windows. He had inspected them closely, only to find the window frames had swollen over time with the weather and neglect. He could not open them. He could only hope to break the glass, and that was not a possibility when at least two of the men were always present.

Jaxcy grew tired. She was beginning to have trouble breathing, her chest hurting with each breath. She couldn't think, not with the pain she was in, and her high fever. Brennen had tried to lower it with cold cloths at night, but it didn't work for long. He had begged for medication to give her, but the men had just looked at him, sneered, and locked the door in front of him.

That last day, Jaxcy stumbled through her chores, not even aware of what she was doing, long moments spent trying to catch her breath and think of what she had to do next. She knew the men were beginning to be freer in their conversation around her, and she wondered at that.

Catching their names, she listened closely even as she worked on the meal. She drew in her breath as best she could. They were planning on taking them away on the Sunday. That was only a couple of days away, she knew. Out of the country, they said. Where? She drew in her breath again, pretending to be busy. She knew of that island. People went there and never returned. She had heard talk of it.

Shoved back into the room, she fell into Brennen's waiting arms, not seeing how he was feeling, that he was trying hard to stay strong for her and failing. He swept her close, dropping to the floor, to just hold her, feeling the heat from her fever through his shirt. Desperate to escape, Brennen finally laid her down and rose, pacing the room once more, the light growing dim as dusk approached. He headed for the door, his hand twisting the knob, not expecting it to turn under his hand and the door open. He paused, listening.

Turning at last, Brennen gathered Jaxcy close to his heart and crept out, down the hallway, to the door that led to the outside, listening for footsteps coming after him. He frowned. He didn't hear the men and he usually could, their voices were that loud.

Creeping slowly across the yard, Brennen headed for a path, or laneway, he wasn't quite sure what to call it. He listened carefully, not hearing anything, his eyes on his beloved princess. He moved forward, step after step, each step a momentous task.

He finally was stopped by men, and he grew afraid, ready to turn and run.

"Brennen? Are you okay? Talk to me." Breck's voice was kept low.

"Breck? You're here? Did they kidnap you too?" Brennen was confused.

Breck gave a low laugh. "No, we're not captive. And it doesn't look as if you are anymore. Here, let me have Jaxcy." Breck waited for a moment for Brennen to respond before he simply gathered Jaxcy into his arms, the other two men stepping up to help Brennen.

They moved quickly back the way that they had just emerged along the trail, heading for the SUV. Breck tucked Jaxcy inside and turned, a frown on his face.

Brennen was protesting, trying to turn back the way that they had just come, insistent that Jaxcy was back there, that he had lost her. He pleaded with them to let him go. Breck shook his head and watched as Brennen was shoved onto a seat beside Jaxcy.

The men watched as Brennen realized Jaxcy was there and gathered her to him, tears on his face as he murmured quietly before he too was lost to them. Their emotions hard to control, they had seated themselves and watched the area as Burnie drove away, heading for the paved road and home.

"I didn't expect you back so soon." Burnie glanced at the seat behind him.

"We met them heading our way. I have no idea how or where they came from."

"The old Smothers' place. It's that way. It's the one Brandon had pinpointed."

"I know. I wonder if Dallas has checked it out." Breck shifted so he could watch the two in the low light inside the vehicle. "They have had it rough, by the looks of it. Jaxcy is sick."

"She's got a high fever." Benen's voice held the concern he didn't want to admit to.

"I know. I could feel it. Pray that Doc and Brady can treat her. I don't want to think of what could happen if we have to take her to the hospital."

Burnie was soon pulling into the loading dock at the building, the SUV in park and the motor shut off. He was out of the vehicle, as were the other men, watching as Doc and Brady approached with the stretchers. They all helped to move the couple to them and then followed as they were moved quickly to the infirmary.

Breck stood beside Barnabas, shaking his head at a question.

"Breck?"

"We found them walking towards us, Barnabas. I don't know how. It was as if Brennen was determined to walk all the way back here."

"And he would have. Go with them. We'll meet shortly." Barnabas rubbed at his face. "It's late. The five of us will meet, the rest of us in the morning." He walked towards the building infirmary. "I'll speak with her parents in the morning, once we know more. I don't like her looks."

"No, she's struggling to breathe. Brennen is worn out. He looks as if he's been beaten again. She's been beaten too. Who does this?" Breck was worried and frustrated.

"We'll find then, Breck. We'll find them. We need to keep these two safe, and just how we do that, I'm not sure anymore."

# Chapter 38

Brennen finally stopped speaking, his eyes on Jaxcy, wishing it had been different. She had not needed to be taken captive, to be forced to perform what amounted to slave labour. He had not shared with the group what Jaxcy had told him in the infirmary. Her parents didn't need to hear that. He had spoken to Dallas about it, who had frowned at him and then nodded.

"Brennen?" He looked up at Bruce. "What else?"

The younger man shrugged. "Not a whole lot. I was basically looked up in the room, except when Jaxcy was in the kitchen. They wanted me there at that point for some reason."

"Intimidation towards her. If they threatened you, she would do what they wanted." Barnabas shared a look with Breck. They knew Brennen. They knew that he was holding something back. "Look, you need to get your wife to bed. She's still sick. And you need your rest." Barnabas stood, the others rising as well. "Don't get up, Brennen. I'll be back in the morning. Call me or Breck, if you need to."

Brennen nodded, weary to his bones, he thought. He just sat, his eyes on Jaxcy before he moved, rising with difficulty, to carry her through to her bed, covering her tightly with the blankets, watching as Kerry jumped up and cuddled close to her.

"It's okay, Kerry. I feel the same way. I don't want her out of my sight." He paused for a moment before he headed for the office, pulling up his email, and scanning it. He sent a quick email off to the publisher, begging his forgiveness for not responding, but giving a shortened version of what had happened. He smiled at the quick email back. The Christian publisher that he worked for knew the men of the Foundation building, had been a frequent guest of Barnabas and the board.

Brennen finally pulled his phone towards him. He could not sleep without talking to either Barnabas or Breck. Breck won on the call.

"Brennen? I thought you would be calling." Breck shifted back in his easy chair, a hand automatically reaching for the pad of paper and pen he kept on the table beside it.

"Thanks, once more, Breck, for what you fellows did. I know. You don't want thanks, but you have it anyway." Brennen paused, not quite sure how to continue.

"What didn't you say, Brennen? What was it that you felt you could not be open with in front of her parents?"

"What? You're reading my mind?" Brennen grinned for a moment at Breck's laughter before he sobered. "There is something. You told me that her parents had been sent overseas. Did they know they were being sent?"

"That's an interesting question. Burnie asked them that. They said no. They had been given something, didn't know they had left Canada until they woke up on the island. There was no way off for them. Very few inhabitants, mostly prisoners, from what we can determine. Abe has not said how difficult it was to get in and out, but I am sure it was. Jeremiah mentioned armed guards."

"Ouch. No, Abe won't say. Nathaniel said they never do. It's not important in their mind. It's the people that are important."

"That is so true. It's been the same with all of you fellows, when Barnabas had had the opportunity to do just that with you twelve. You are there for each other as well." Breck paused to sip at his cold cup of coffee, grimacing at the taste. "But there is more. I know you."

"There is. I didn't want to frighten Jeremiah or Jemma, now that Jaxcy and they are together. Jaxcy mentioned something the other night. She didn't say anything when we were still captive. And I can't figure out why the door was left open, in order for us to escape."

"It had to be done on purpose, Brennen. There is no other explanation. Which one of the men didn't fit in?"

"I would say the driver. He would be around once in a while." Brennen groaned. "And he was there that day. The men had to leave to meet with someone. He always appeared when they needed a ride. He could have had the opportunity to unlock the door on the way out. We were not that far from the outside door."

"Okay, so, someone there is playing both sides. How do we find him?"

"I don't think we will. I would imagine that he is either dead or has disappeared on his own. They were too vicious for it to be anything else." Brennen grew silent, a prayer raised for that man. "But, that's not what I needed to say. When Jaxcy awakened in the infirmary, she thought we were still captive. She asked what the day was. She had overheard plans to send us overseas on Sunday. They were planning on sending us out of the country."

"I see." Breck paused, his thoughts running ahead of his ability to form words. "Do you think they were planning on the same island, now that you know?"

"I doubt it. They would not want Jaxcy to know her parents were alive. I would suspect an island close to there." Brennen caught himself yawning. "I need to go, Breck, but I needed you or Barnabas to know this tonight."

"I'll make sure I tell him. Have a good night's sleep, Brennen. You two are in our prayers." Breck had risen, hearing the apartment door open, and seeing Barnabas in his kitchen. He set his phone down on the kitchen table, taking the mug of coffee offered to him with thanks.

"Brennen?" Barnabas nodded towards the phone.

"It was. He called with some additional information. Jaxcy overheard a plot to send them overseas last Sunday."

"Overseas? Not to the same island, I doubt. They wouldn't know yet, I don't think, that Jaxcy's parents are here."

"I think they do. Eric has mentioned seeing evidence that the building has been watched. It's happening all over again. I thought we told Brendon it stopped with him?"

"We did, but it doesn't seem to work. We need to make some plans, and then meet with the men in the morning."

"They're all pulling back from their work until we can get this solved. Brennen has gone above and beyond for each of them. They want to repay in some small way that favour."

"He has. It's his character. Now, where do we stand, and what do we do? Dad's hanging around for a couple of days. He'll want to be in on the planning." Barnabas reached for a pad of paper and pen, laughing at Breck's apology for having one waiting for him.

# Chapter 39

The next afternoon, Jaxcy stood where Brennen could not see her as he worked away at the kitchen table, his ever-present mug of coffee beside him. She had just awakened and rising, had wandered through the apartment looking for him. She watched as Kerry stood up at him, sniffing at his face, receiving a hug and a good rubbing on his head from Brennen.

Brennen raised his head, to stare across the room. Blair had been around, dropping off material for him to look through. He was impressed at the amount of work that had accumulated the pile of papers in front of him. But, then again, it was how they worked. Brennen had nodded at Blair's request to call when he spotted anything unusual. The thing was, he thought, that he wouldn't know what was unusual or different.

A hand held out behind him, he spoke softly to Jaxcy.

"Hi, Princess. Have a good sleep?"

"I guess. You should have awakened me." She clasped his hand, feeling him pull her towards him and down on his knee.

"You needed to sleep. Feeling any better?"

"I guess." She sighed. "That seems to be the extent of my vocabulary." She poked at the papers. "What is this?"

"Research from the fellows. I am not sure where they were headed with what they have here."

Jaxcy leafed through it. "They have really dug deep. This is Aunt Jackie. This is Uncle Joseph." She sorted through the material, setting it into different piles. "But what is this?"

"That? I wondered at that. The names? Do you recognize them?"

"No, I don't. I have not seen names like that in any of our family histories. Mom and Dad might recognize them."

"Someone will ask them, I am sure." Brennen's head tilted to watch her. "How do we solve this, Jaxcy? And how do we keep you safe?"

"You too." Her voice was barely a whisper. "We need to keep you safe too, Brennen. I can't lose you."

His arms tightened around her. "Nor I, you. So, what do we do?"

"I can't stay inside all the time, Brennen. It will kill me. I need to be outside, working in the earth. Do you understand?"

"I do. It's part of who you are. All we can do is be as cautious as we can, and pray lots."

"Yeah, well, that. It doesn't seem to be working too well."

"We are alive, Princess. God has kept us alive. Sure, we have been through stuff, been hurt. You're sick. But God has been there."

"I know." She sighed. "It's just so hard." Her voice died away as she stared at the papers. "Brennen, what if Dad and Mom didn't set up the trust fund? That has puzzled me all along. They never had extra money. Their parents were not rich. There were no rich relatives, not that I am aware of."

Brennen's hand froze for a moment before he reached for his pen and then he flipped over one of the pieces of paper. "Okay. We've assumed all along that it was them. If you're right, and I suspect that you are, who would have done this?"

"That's what I have been trying to think about. Someone known to Aunt Jackie? Uncle Joseph? He disappeared so many years ago. What if it wasn't someone from the town, but someone who wanted to set Mom and Dad up for something, and to do that they had to be removed. That way, they could go after me. Get rid of me and then let Mom and Dad come home?" Jaxcy shuddered at the thought. "I don't like the way I'm thinking, Brennen."

"Nor do I, but I think you are on to something." He sorted through the pages. "Here. Brandon mentioned something or someone. He wasn't real clear on it. We need to talk to him."

"Where is he now?"

Brennen glared at the clock. "If he's not working, then he would be in the conference room." He reached for his phone, sending off a quick text to Brandon. "He'll come up here, Princess. That way, you can still rest."

"I feel like an invalid." Jaxcy was grumpy and knew she was showing it.

"That you are still, Princess. I know that it's tough. You didn't ask to get sick." He studied her. "I just thank God that we got away and got you to help."

"That's what I don't understand, Brennen. How did we get away?"

"The door was unlocked. We suspect that it was the driver who unlocked the door for us."

"I think that you are correct. He just didn't seem to fit. I thought that he was watching the men too closely, and not us at all."

"You did? You never mentioned that."

"I thought that I had." Jaxcy sighed. "Brennen, have you been receiving messages that don't make sense, that threaten us?"

"I have been. I need to talk to you about them as well. Dallas has them."

"He does? And what does he say?"

"That it's typical to receive them. I know the other fellows did." Brennen hesitated before he spoke. "Princess, I need to ask you something. Are you happy living here?"

She turned to him, surprised at his question. "I am. You're here. I am making the friends that I could never make in my hometown. Why do you ask?"

"Because when you were in the infirmary, you asked me to take you home. I thought it meant back east."

Jaxcy gave a sad smile. "Did I? And you've been trying to figure out how to do just that? Oh, Brennen, no. This is our home. I don't think I ever want to go back there."

Brennen breathed a sigh of relief. "Well, I guess that's that, then. We stay here. I'll talk to Barnabas, if you like, about your place. He'll look after it for you." He frowned as his phone chimed. "It's Brandon. He's on his way up here."

Jaxcy was off Brennen's knee and heading for the bedroom. "I need to get dressed then."

Brennen stared after her, realizing that she really had been in her dressing gown. He shook his head even as he headed for the door to answer the knock. He was losing it, wasn't he, Lord?

# Chapter 40

Brandon stared at Jaxcy for a moment, realizing that she had pinpointed something that he knew the men had overlooked. He sighed, before he looked at Brennen, finding his attention on Jaxcy.

"Jaxcy? Did you have to complicate our search?" Brandon shook his finger at her.

Jaxcy started at him, her eyes narrowing as she caught the grin that he was trying hard to hide. "You fellows needed my help, obviously. It's only logical that it had to be someone outside the family. How do we find them, and then how do we prove it? I can tell you how to use natural stuff for fertilizers and how to grow plants. This I can't do." Her finger flicked at the papers in front of her.

"But you see, you have. You sorted through this, didn't you?" Brandon looked at the piles. "Your aunt, your uncle, others. But what is this pile?"

"That? Those people? I have no idea who they are or how they fit in. They are not from my town. I can tell you that much." Jaxcy looked up as Brennen gave a small sound. "Brennen?"

"Jaxcy, the man from the bank? The one we connected to Smithers? What was his name?"

"Wayne Johnston. Why?" She leaned against as she looked at the list he had compiled. "He's there and you have his brother, son, nephew, daughter, sister, cousin. Who don't you have?"

"That's what I am wondering." Brennen stared at her as she sat back, her gaze intense as she stared at Brandon.

"Jaxcy?" Brandon's voice stirred her to shake her head.

"Brandon? Did you come across anything that showed their relatives from another province? I think they had family out west."

"As in British Columbia? Where your aunt is?" Brennen watched as her face paled. "I am not saying that she is involved. Did your aunt marry?"

"She had been. That I remember. But I don't remember her husband. I can't remember if he died, they divorced, or if one of them just walked out on the other. Mom or Dad would know."

Brandon had been sorting through the pile of papers on her aunt. He read the bottom paper and looked up. "He died, under suspicious circumstances out west. The police felt that he was killed, but they could not prove it. It says here that your aunt remarried within a month of his death."

"That quick? Wow!" Jaxcy reached for the paper and then paled as she read the name. "This is a cousin to Johnston. How?"

"That we will ask." Brandon pulled out his phone, a finger in the air to pause her questions, as he read his text. A stern look crossed his face, one that Brennen recognized.

"Brandon? Where is she?"

Jaxcy stared between the two men, not quite sure what was being asked.

Brennen's hand reached for hers. "Your aunt isn't out west anymore, Jaxcy. I would hazard a guess that she is in our vicinity."

"She is. Emma just sent word to Brady. Your aunt and her husband have been seen in the area. Together with the Smothers' family. That is where you were held, at one of their properties. They are not even trying to hide it anymore, Brennen."

"I know. That scares me, Brandon." Brennen leaned forward, a frown on his face. "So, if they are not hiding it, what is their plan? And how do we combat it?"

The men spent some time discussing their thoughts, Jaxcy noting down the highlights before a train of thought sidetracked her. She rose, heading for the office, searching for a map, returning to the table to unfurl it.

Brennen watched her closely, not quite sure what she was up to.

"Jaxcy?"

"Okay. I'm not sure how to really say what I need to, so I just have to talk." She paused, gathering her breath, knowing it was taking a lot from her just to speak. "This is a map of Canada. You are all from different provinces and territories? Am I correct?" At their nod, she pointed. "This is where I am from. Aunt Jackie moved across the country years ago, before

Mom and Dad disappeared. They were taken to an island in the Southern Hemisphere, at least, I think that is where. Suppose someone on the west coast needed to set up on the east coast? How would they do that?"

Brennen and Brandon exchanged glances.

"I think you are onto something, Jaxcy. And using the property next to us? Saying it was yours? That would implicate you in whatever it was they are planning. We are readily available to Lake Erie and then through the canal system, to Lake Ontario and then the Atlantic Ocean." Brandon was on his feet, gathering their papers. "Are you well enough to come downstairs, Jaxcy?"

She shrugged, knowing that she wasn't, but she was determined to end this. "I will be. I want this over, for Brennen's sake. And for my parents. Enough time has been stolen from our family."

# Chapter 41

Approaching Brennen, Bradon and Burnie sat on either side of him. Jaxcy had gone to stand in front of the map, her finger tracing the area that Brendon was pointing out to her.

"Brennen? What's up?"

"Jaxcy has come up with an interesting idea. She asked Brandon and me if someone wanted to expand their criminal activities to the east coast, how would they do that?"

His two friends exchanged glances.

"She's right, you know. That trust fund? Laundered money? It was never meant to go to her." Burnie paled. "Does she still have it?"

Brennen shook his head. "No. We turned all the information over to Dallas, and he has had the Foundation attorney look into it. It never really existed."

"It didn't? You two went through all this for nothing?" Bradon shook his head.

"No, it's not for nothing." Brennen was trying to understand what was going on and then explain it. "It was a setup. What we haven't had a chance to tell you fellows is that our captors planned to ship us out of the country, just like her parents."

"And no one would have ever found you?" Bradon paused. "Who?"

"That's what we need to determine. In the paperwork that Brandon gave me, it showed that her aunt had remarried and that they are in the area. We are not sure why."

"When did they arrive?" Burnie was on his feet, heading for his own chair, returning with a sheaf of papers. "Is it in these?"

Brennen took them, quickly finding what he wanted. "Here. This is what we found. We need to talk to the officers out west."

"Dallas can do that." Bradon was on his feet, moving away, his phone out to call Dallas. He turned to watch Jaxcy, seeing the fatigue that she was trying hard to hide, the whiteness of her face a sharp contrast to the dark shadows under her eyes. We need to solve this, Lord, and soon, he thought.

Breck stood in the doorway, eyeing each one of the men, before his focus stayed on Jaxcy. He moved towards her, watching her closely, seeing just how close to collapse that she was. His hand drew her to a chair near Brennen, before he was away and then back with a cup of tea for her.

"Here, Jaxcy. Drink this. And then, Brennen needs to take you home."

Jaxcy shook her head. "No, I need to stay. Please, Breck? I need to be part of this."

Breck stood for a moment, considering her words before he was out of the room, beckoning for Brady to come with him.

"Brady, she won't leave, and she's almost ready to collapse."

"I know. I was watching her. Even Brennen isn't going to be able to make her leave." Brady headed down the other hallway. "Let's take that cot over for her. At least, that way, she can rest."

"I agree. I was heading for it. What else?"

"Her medications? I think she needs some oxygen as well. Maybe an IV?"

The two men worked quickly, gathering what they needed, meeting Doc as they headed back.

"Brady?"

"Jaxcy is refusing to go back to the apartment. She's in the conference room. We're hoping to get her to rest."

Doc nodded, reaching for some of Brady's burden, before he followed them. He approached Jaxcy, finding her sitting with her eyes closed, her arms wrapped around her. A gentle touch had her jumping and then nodding at Doc's quiet words. He settled her on the cot, oxygen in place, and an IV started. He was worried, he thought. Lord, heal this girl. That young man over there is head over heels in love with her and needs her. Resolve whatever it is that they are going through and soon.

Brennen had lifted his head and watched as Jaxcy settled down on the cot, a relieved sigh rising from him. He had tried to get her to leave, to let him take her home, but she had refused and moved away from him. He turned as Buckley sat beside him.

"Brennen? What's this I hear that they wanted to ship you two out of the country?"

"Jaxcy overheard them. I don't get why, though."

A sound from Branigan had them all turning his way, watching the grimness that began to cover his face. Branigan shot a look at Jaxcy, noting how still she had become.

"Fellows, I think I know why. And I think I know why Jaxcy is so sick. Doc, how sure are you that it's pneumonia?"

"As sure as I can be without X-Rays. Why?"

"If she was exposed to a chemical, would she have symptoms like this?"

Doc paused, his eyes on Branigan, before he nodded. "Maybe not the high fever, but the breathing issues? Yes. Why?"

Branigan was on his feet, heading for Doc, a paper held out. "Check out this. I think she had chemical exposure. Dallas sent over some information, off the record, that puzzled him. He wanted me to talk to Brennen or Jaxcy."

"Is that ethical that he did that?" This from Breck.

Branigan shrugged. "I have no idea. He's bouncing around ideas, he said. And one of them is a chemical that he has heard about on the street. That it would be released into the air and affect many people, allowing the perpetrators to take over a government. He wonders if Jaxcy was a test case."

Brennen's face grew dark with anger. "They did that? Is that why they had her cleaning all the time. She said that they made her clean the whole house every, single day. She didn't think it needed that much cleaning."

"And somehow, somewhere, they exposed her to this." Doc's face grew grave. He spun, searching. "Breck, we need to get some supplies and quickly. I can't tell how serious it is. Is there someone with a portable X-Ray machine?"

Brady lifted his phone. "Already done, Doc. They'll be here in fifteen."

"Good. Now, Breck, come with me. Brady, you stay here. Call me if she worsens or call 911 and take her in."

Chapter 42

Watching as Jaxcy's condition worsened, Brady finally rose, gathering her into his arms, and running for the door, Branigan at his heels, holding the doors for him, and pointing to his truck. Brennen had looked up, thrown down his pen, and ran after them.

"Brady?"

"She's worse, Brennen. I need to take her in. I can't wait for the crew to arrive."

Brennen slid into Branigan's truck, reaching for his bride, cradling her to him, watching as she struggled to breathe.

"Brady?"

"We don't think it's pneumonia, Brennen. Dallas questioned if she had been exposed to any chemicals. I guess they found traces of something."

Brennen paled, even as he kept a watch on her. "And if it is? Can we treat her?"

"That's our plan, Brennen." Brady was monitored Jaxcy as closely as he could. "Unfortunately, I think we'll have to intubate her and place her on a ventilator until we can get the treatment started."

Brennen paled even more before his anger rose. "Find this person or persons. I want to face them, to ask them if a young lady's life was worth it."

"They'll tell you that it was. We'll do our best, Brennen. Buckley will have the church and everyone that he can reach praying for you two."

Three hours later, Brennen looked up as a hand rested on his shoulder. His face was pale and drawn, fear and grief showing on it and in his eyes.

"Doc?"

Doc sat wearily into a chair. He had not been on call but had come in when Brady had alerted him to bringing Jaxcy in. He had fought with the physicians and nurses to save her. So far, they had been successful. Dallas had been around, bringing in what information that the techs had provided him.

"Brennen, we have had a fight. She is not out of the woods yet. Not by a long shot. Dallas has given us what he can. We've found a treatment and have started it. She'll be going up to ICU shortly."

Brennen nodded, already convinced in his mind that he was losing her. Her parents sat beside him, Jemma's arm around him.

"Can I see her?"

"Give us time to get her settled. Head on up, Brennen. I'll meet you there." Doc stood, hesitated for a moment, and then moved away.

Jeremiah watched him walk away. "Brennen? What can we do for you?"

Brennen's head shot around to stare at the older man, surprise on his face. "I'm not sure. I should be asking you that."

Jemma spoke up. "Jaxcy has made it obvious that you are the love of her life, the one that she was waiting for. We need to keep you healthy, Brennen. She will survive this. She will need you when she awakes."

Brennen rose, staring down at the fingers that he was rubbing together. "I guess. I wish I had your optimism and faith." He pointed to the elevator. "Let's head up there. Doc will find us."

Jeremiah's arm was around his wife, knowing that she was grieving already, thinking that they had found their daughter once more, only to lose her.

Brennen paced the waiting room late that night. He had sent Jeremiah and Jemma home finally, stating that he would call. He had no idea who still remained of his friends, but he knew some had. He turned to face the doors to the ICU rooms before he shook his head. It wasn't time yet that he could go back in. Brennen knew that the staff was working their magic or whatever you wanted to call it to keep his princess alive. He was losing hope that they would.

Doc stood and watched his young friend. He shook his head. Why, Lord? Why have all these young men and ladies gone through life and death struggles? I just don't get it. But You are in control. That much I know. Please, Lord, give us the wisdom that we need to treat this young lady. She is responding, I know, dear Lord, but not quite how we would expect her. He paused, feeling his phone vibrating. He pulled it out. Bruce Carey was on the phone, stating that he had found someone to come in and consult. Did they want him? He had courtesy privileges at the hospital and was an expert in chemical contamination.

Doc breathed a sigh of relief. He had not even asked for that, and the Lord had provided.

"Yes, Bruce. We could use his expertise with Jaxcy. We're treating her but we need more information."

"That's what I thought you would say. He should be there in ten minutes. I told him to ask for you or Terry."

"Thank you. We need to find the treatment we need for Jaxcy." He turned to watch Brennen. "I could use someone to talk with Brennen. Do we know anyone?"

"I'll see who I can track down." Bruce was gone before Doc could even say anything. He turned to speak with Brennen, instead seeing a tall, distinguished man walking his way.

"I'm looking for Doctor Andrews."

"That would be me. And you would be?" Doc reached to shake his hand.

"I'm Jake Webster. Bruce Carey sent me your way. Said you needed some assistance with diagnosing and treating a young lady." Jake turned slightly as he heard footsteps behind him.

"That we do." Doc's hand reached to draw Brennen close. "This is Brennen, Jaxcy's husband. They were kidnapped a few days ago. Jaxcy has been running a high fever but developed breathing difficulties. We assumed it was pneumonia but she became much worse today. We brought her in. Right now, she's on a ventilator."

Brennen studied the physician standing in front of him, a frown on his face. He looked familiar, but he could not place him.

"Dr. Webster? What can you do for my princess?" Brennen's desperation came through in his voice.

"I'll what I can do, young man. What can you tell me?" His keen eyes studied Brennen closely.

"Not a lot. She was made to clean the house where we were kept every day, even though it didn't need it. We think she might have been exposed to something. The last day, she could barely function."

"I see. Dr. Andrews? Where is this young lady? And what else can you tell me?" His hand stopped Brennen from moving away, drawing him with them towards Jaxcy's room. "I want this young man with us. He may have information that we need, without being aware of it."

An hour later, Doc stood back, watching Jaxcy closely, breathing a sigh of relief. Jake had thrown off his jacket, rolled up his sleeves, and plunged right into determining what Jaxcy was exposed to, based on the information provided by Dallas earlier. He had questioned Brennen extensively as well, drawing from him details that had not been provided earlier, simply because no one had known the questions to ask.

Brennen stood beside the bed, his hand on Jaxcy's face, his own face white and drawn. He was beginning to weave from the fatigue that was crippling him. Doc caught him as he collapsed, Jake reaching to help, drawing up the chair that had been provided for them.

Doc crouched down beside Brennen, assessing him before he looked up at Jake.

"Has he been exposed to the chemical?"

"More than likely, I would say. Can you run blood work and ask for them to check for that particular chemical, just as we did for Jaxcy?"

"I can. Terry will be around shortly as well, he said." Doc stood. "I just don't get it."

"Get what? Their exposure? This particular chemical is manufactured in an illegal lab, used for criminal activities. I have no idea why they were exposed, though. It is usually part of criminal activities overseas."

Doc paled. "And there's your answer. Jaxcy mentioned that the plan was to take them out of the country. But if they were testing it on them, that doesn't make a lot of sense."

"No, it doesn't. Now, let's have a look at this young man."

# Chapter 43

Looking up the next morning, from where he was seated in the waiting room, Brennen stared at the man standing in the doorway, watching him. He frowned, started to rise, and then stopped as the man turned and walked away. That was strange, he thought. Who was that?

Branigan stared after the man, thinking he looked familiar but not sure why. He headed towards Brennen, handing him a takeout cup of coffee and a bag containing a muffin.

"Doc said you hadn't eaten." Branigan dropped down beside him.

"No, I haven't. Thanks, Branigan." He sipped at the coffee, before setting it aside to open the bag and pull out the muffin. "Where is everyone else?"

"Hard at work, trying to figure out who is responsible for all this." Branigan nodded towards the door to the unit. "How is Jaxcy?"

"Better, much better. Bruce found someone who could come in and treat her. Whatever he found to treat her has worked. Doc and Terry think they'll be able to pull the ventilator later today. Doc isn't supposed to be up here, not being an Emergency physician, but they have allowed him to do just that."

"I wondered. I know Terry has been glad of his assistance." Branigan's eyes closed for a moment. He had been up all night, working away on trying to track down Jaxcy's uncle. "I have a line on her uncle."

"You do? And?" Brennen waited for Branigan to speak.

"He's not in Canada. As far as we can determine, he moved to the United Kingdom years ago and has not been back since."

"I see. Does Jeremiah know that?"

"Not yet." Branigan peered around Branigan, seeing Breck and Brody heading their way. "Barnabas said he'd talk to him."

Breck and Brody waited for Brennen to speak, sharing a glance when he didn't. Neither were sure just why he didn't.

"Brennen?"

Brennen's head shot up, surprise on his face. "I didn't see you two. I'm sorry." His eyes slid closed for a moment, fatigue weighing them down.

"How is Jaxcy?" Breck was almost afraid to ask.

"Better. Thank you for the prayers. She is better." Brennen's eyes caught the nurse approaching, and he was on his feet, a muttered excuse me thrown at the men, before he was striding rapidly towards her. "Nurse?"

She smiled. "It's okay, Brennen. Terry asked me to come and find you. He needs to update you." Her hand on his arm stopped his forward movement. "They pulled the ventilator already. She is breathing on her own, with just oxygen by nasal prongs."

"She is? Oh, thank God." Brennen almost hugged her before he was away, striding down the hall, a lighter movement to his steps.

Breck had risen and watched him move away from them. "That must have been good news."

Two days later, Jaxcy sat cross-legged on the bed, dressed in leggings and a heavy sweater. She had been allowed to be up and moving around, no longer needing the oxygen. Fynn and Imly watched her closely, trying to read how she was. Imly finally just approached her, sat on the bed, and reached for her hands, her head bowing as she prayed for her friend.

Jaxcy wiped the tears that had fallen on her cheeks. "Thank you, Imly." Her voice was still a hoarse whisper. "You have no idea what this means for me."

"I think I do. We have all had to go through things that we could never have imagined. We have formed a close group. We want you to be part of that. That being said, when are they springing you?"

Fynn laughed at the expression. "Imly? Really?"

Imly just grinned. "I know. Darbie and the twins are corrupting my language, aren't they?"

Jaxcy smiled, content suddenly with the knowledge that she was a welcome part of a group, no longer an outcast, to wait on the sidelines. She no longer had to long to belong. She did.

"Terry said tomorrow. I'm just afraid, ladies. I am afraid that whoever it is will come after Brennen."

"I know what you mean." Fynn dropped into a chair. "Now, the other ladies are planning on preparing meals for now for you two. Brennen said that he needs to work, he has a couple of books waiting for him."

"I know he does. I told him to stay away today and work on them. He hasn't listened to me." Jaxcy caught sight of Brennen in the doorway.

Brennen laughed as he approached, bending to hug and kiss her.

"You did, and I did, but I needed to be here. Terry called. He wanted to talk to us." He looked up as Fynn and Imly started to rise. "It's okay, ladies. You can stay, if you wish. Jaxcy and I talked it over. We can't hide what happened, and if you being here will help us solve this, then we welcome you here."

Fynn and Imly exchanged a glance before they looked at Jaxcy, seeing her smile of agreement.

"You know, you fellows have not asked us for any input." Imly grinned at the look on Brennen's face as he realized how true that was.

"You are so right." Brennen looked at Fynn. "Fynn, what would you suggest?"

"I suggest that we blow this joint, taking Jaxcy with us." She pointed to the door, where Terry stood, waving papers at them. "Here are her discharge papers. At least, I think that's what Terry is waving at us."

# Chapter 44

Staring down at the papers that he was holding, Brandon could not believe what he was reading. He turned, searching the room, not seeing Brennen around.

"Where's Brennen?" His call raised the heads of the men who had gathered in the room.

"Brennen? He said that he had some work to do. Why?" Benen was on his feet, heading for Brandon.

"Because I think I just figured out who is involved." Brandon shoved the paper at Benen. "Are you seeing what I'm seeing?"

Benen stared at his friend for a moment, before he took the paper that Brandon kept shoving at him.

"What are you talking about?"

"Read it. Tell me if you see what I see." Brandon pointed at the paper, turning his head as he heard the door open and close. "Brennen? Take a look at this."

"At what?" Brennen walked wearily across the room. He had moved Jaxcy home the day before, settled her that morning in their living room with some of the ladies, and then headed to work. He had needed a break, he thought, and had headed to the conference room. "What are you talking about?"

"Here." Benen handed him the papers, his face grim as he nodded at Brandon. "I see it, Brandon. I think that you are correct. In fact, that correlates with what I just found." He turned, hurrying back to where he had been seated, and printing off the work he had just done. "Here. This goes with that."

The other men had gathered around them, exchanging glances, not quite sure what was going on, but knowing Brandon and Benen had made a discovery.

Brennen rubbed at his eyes and then his forehead, a headache growing that he refused to take anything for.

"What?" He stared at the paper, and then looked up at Benen. "Him? She trusted him. He's the only one that she really trusted in her town."

"I know. But he had the perfect cover, now didn't he? Who would suspect a minister?" Brandon looked around as snickers from the men filled the room. "Sorry, Buckley. We know you're honest."

"Well, I guess I have to say thanks then, I think." Buckley reached for the paper, a frown. "Her minister? Wait a moment. That's not the name she gave."

"No, he has been using a different name. He played her, Brennen, and well. And I doubt that he is as old as she thinks he is."

"No, I don't think so. He had to have known who I was. He's the one who sent me the letter, that much Jaxcy and I figured out." Brennen sank down into a chair, his elbow bracing his head. "Where do we go with this?"

"Here. Emma just sent some information that goes with that." Brady handed a sheaf of papers to each man. "She said that she suspected him, but had to do some digging. He's been involved in a lot of criminal activities on the sly, she says."

"And her parents would have trusted him enough to take what he offered in food or drink. That's how they did it." Brendon spun, heading for the map. "Let's see. Emma says that he was from this area, just north of us a way. There." His finger found the spot of a small town. "And guess what? That's where we tracked both Smithers and the Smothers families to."

Brennen stared at the paper, not really reading it, a frown in place. "Are you saying that they are all from the same town? How did we miss that?"

"I don't think that we did." Blair spoke up. "It wasn't until you too were kidnapped and then we found you on the Smothers' property that it all began to gel. Now, what do we do about it?"

"Set a trap." The men turned to stare at Devaney as she moved into their midst. "Trap them. I have no idea. You fellows always have such great ideas. But draw them out. Bring them together."

"She's right. That may be what we have to do." Blair wrapped an arm around his wife. "Is the minister around here?"

"He is. Emma says that they have tracked him to our town. He arrived, when?" Brody looked at his paperwork. "The day before you two were kidnapped, Brennen."

"So, he has to be involved. But who is behind it all? Someone has to be, to have access to the chemicals needed to manufacture what they tested on Jaxcy." Brennen rose and began pacing. "Where do we go from here?"

# Chapter 45

Jaxcy stared at Brennen and then Burnie, listening carefully to their explanation of who was involved and how. She shook her head and then waved her hand at them to stop their talking.

"Johnny? I don't see that. He's old."

"Actually, Jaxcy, he's not. He played old, but he's around your father's age." Brennen sank beside her, an arm around her.

"He is? I wouldn't have guessed that. So, if he is, he knew all along that you would show up. Why you?"

"That is something that we will ask him." Burnie held up a finger as he pulled out his phone, frowning at the text message. "I guess that we won't after all. Breck just sent out a text. They pulled the minister's body from the lake this afternoon."

"Getting rid of the ones who could bring their organization down?" Brennen sighed. "So, we're back to square one, I gather."

"Not necessarily." Burnie held up the folder that he had dropped onto the coffee table. "This is some of the research that we have done. Some that Emma has sent us. In it, I think we will find the answers. Or at least, I pray we do." He handed it over to Jaxcy. "Jaxcy. You know your town. Read through it. Tell us what you think." He grinned as he handed over pens and highlighters. "Mark that copy up all you want."

“I can. Okay.” Jaxcy began to read, a frown of concentration on her face.

Brennen pointed to the kitchen, motioning Burnie to come with him. He reached into the fridge, a glance at the clock showing it was lunchtime. Burnie worked with him, preparing a simple meal.

“Will she find something, Brennen?” Burnie glanced towards the living room.

Brennen stepped to where he could watch her, finding her staring into space, her hand upraised with a pen in it.

“I think that she has. Give her some time. She needs to think through it all. Then, she’ll tell us what she thinks.” Brennen shook his head. “I hate this, Burnie. Whoever this is has been her family through a horrible experience.”

“And it’s hard not to hate them, isn’t it?” Burnie studied his friend. “All the other fellows have struggled with that as well.”

“I guess.” Brennen stood for a moment, staring out the kitchen window. “It’s just so hard not to.”

“Hard not to do what?” Jaxcy’s arm came around him, her question turning his face towards her.

“Not to hate whoever is responsible.”

Jaxcy nodded. “I know, Brennen. It is hard. You have no idea of the number of hours that I have spent asking for the hate to be taken away. I have had to do that for so many years.” She looked up at Burnie. “Burnie, I think that I have an answer for you. But we need to talk to everyone else." She swayed for a moment, fatigue hitting her.

"You, Princess, need to rest for a bit. Here, let's eat in the living room. Then, you can stretch out on the couch and tell us exactly what you have found."

Brennen and Burnie stared dumbfounded at Jaxcy an hour later as she finished her summation of the findings that she had discovered. Brennen reached for the papers that she had dropped to the floor, sorting through them, reading her notes. He sighed.

"You have complicated it, Princess."

"No, I have not. I have clarified it." She shot him a mutinous look, then glared at Burnie as he choked back a laugh. "Laugh all you want, Burnie. But this is what I think. You asked me that." A hurt tone sounded in her voice.

Brennen sighed, moving to sit beside her and gather her close. "It's okay, Princess. We believe you. I just don't see how we missed this or missed naming that person."

"Because you don't know the town. I don't know it as well as I should. And if you ask Mom or Dad, they won't know what has happened or the dynamics of the town in the last eleven years. It has changed that much." She pointed at the papers. "And that person and their family are responsible for that. They have relatives all over Canada, their family is that large."

"I see." Burnie reached for the papers, reading her notes. "I see some names that we had looked at, but we didn't have that connection." He looked up, a grin on his face. "I nominate you as lead detective."

"Save that for a book, Burnie. By the time we'll all done, you'll have more fodder than you know what to do with in a novel." Brennen shook his head, feeling Jaxcy's body relaxing, and looking down at her. "She's asleep, Burnie. This has taken too much from her." He studied the thinness and paleness of her face, the black shadows under her eyes.

"It has. She's so petite to begin with, Brennen." Burnie watched her closely. "Is she recovering okay?"

"Terry seemed to think she would. She still needs oxygen every once in a while. We have to monitor her oxygen stats all the time. We won't know for a while if there has been any permanent damage."

"We are all praying that there isn't." Burnie's eyes closed for a moment before they popped open again. "So, what do we do with this?"

"Take it to the fellows. Let them start what they need to. I want to confront these people, and I know that I'll be fought on that."

"Not necessarily, Brennen." Burnie nodded towards Jaxcy. "We'll all be there. I'm off then. One of us will be by later to update you." With that, Burnie was gone, the apartment door closing quietly behind him.

# Chapter 46

Two days later, Brennen approached Breck, a quiet question asked, and then he walked away. Breck stared after him, not quite sure what Brennen was up to, before he was running after him, a hand out to stop him.

"Brennen? What did you just ask me?"

"I asked you how well does Bruce know that specialist that he sent in?" Brennen was puzzled.

"I can ask. Bruce knows so many people."

"I know, but it's just strange how all of a sudden he appeared. I know Bruce does this, but I have to question that physician."

Breck nodded. "I know. I would do the same. Let me talk to Bruce, find out what I can. You'll be around?"

"I have to head to town for a bit. I need to do some research in the library." Brennen paused at the look on Breck's face. "What? You don't think I should?"

"It would likely be best if someone went with you. They'll try and take you again, just to get to Jaxcy. She has to know something or someone."

"I think that she has given everything that she can. She's still not healing well, Breck. I want to find someone else for her to see."

"Leave it with me. I'll find you someone." Breck watched as Brennen walked away, a stoop to his shoulders that was unusual. He's wearing out, Lord, and we need to help him. Only, I don't see how.

Bruce Carey stared at Breck thirty minutes later as the younger man stood in front of him. Bruce had still been around the building, and Breck had tracked him down.

"He asked what exactly?" Bruce knew Brennen well enough to know that it was not an idle question.

"He just asked how well you know the physician that stepped in." Breck was hesitant to speak, not wanting to shed any wrong on the physician.

"I see. Not that well. We've met at meetings and he is on the board of a local hospice. I can see why Brennen would ask." Bruce paced away and then back. "You know, it is strange. He approached me, asking how the men were." He stared hard at Breck, an inscrutable look on his face. "He specifically asked about Brennen."

Breck nodded. "There's our connection then. Bruce, we need to research this. Come with me."

Bruce's hand was out to stop him. "Your office, Breck. We keep this between us until we find out for sure."

"Of course. That's where I was heading." Breck sighed as his phone chimed and he pulled it out. "That's strange. It's an email from Emma." His face paled. "Bruce, it's about that physician."

"That's not good. What does she say?"

"That he is up on disciplinary measures, has been relieved of his duties and privileges at all the hospitals, including ours." Breck looked up, shock on his face. "He should never have been in there, treating her. She goes on to say that the authorities from out west, Alberta, are looking for him in connection with criminal activities that he has been connected to." He groaned.

"And it has to do with chemical warfare?" Bruce took a guess.

"It does. I just wish this was over. Brennen stated that he wants to find another physician to assess Jaxcy."

"And that I will do, personally." Bruce sat in front of Breck's desk. "Okay, Breck. Let's start our research. We need to prove this, and then get that proof to that young Dallas."

Two hours later, Breck tidied the papers that he had printed into a neat pile and looked up at Bruce.

"I think that we have what we need."

"I do as well. You head off to find Dallas. I'll find the men. I would assume that they are in the conference room?" Bruce grinned, knowing the men too well.

"The ones that can be are. The ladies were taking turns with Jaxcy, as much as she will let them."

"Her parents?"

"They have been in and out. They don't want to settle in the building. And I can't say as I blame them."

"No, I don't. If they are looking for a place in town, send them to Sally. She'll find them one of our houses." Bruce was away before Breck could respond.

Breck waited for Dallas to approach him, a frown on his face as he studied the top paper. Bruce and he had determined so much, but would it be enough? He knew Dallas would have to confirm everything.

"Breck? The duty officer said you needed to speak with me?" Dallas waited for Breck to speak.

"I do. Bruce and I took a question that Brennen asked and did a lot of research." He handed over the folder. "Here. This is on the physician that came in and treated Jaxcy. He's involved."

"He is? Sandy was getting red flags on him, but had to set it aside." Dallas glanced quickly through the material. "I don't know how you all do this. You find information that we don't."

"Like it's been said before. You think like a police officer. We don't. Just a different perspective."

"And that is true. Thanks, Breck. Watch Brennen and Jaxcy." Dallas looked up when Breck didn't respond and then groaned. "No, they're not, are they?"

"Brennen wants to confront them. He's working on a plan, I just know. I only hope that he informs us of what he is planning."

"I do too. Let me know what it is and I'll make sure that he's protected."

# Chapter 47

The next day, Jaxcy wandered the rose garden, unable to stay inside. Cadee, Ennis, and Guenivere were with her. She was tired, she thought. Tired of what they were going through, tired of scrimping and saving, a habit that Brennen was trying his best to get her to break, but it is so hard, she thought. Lord, when will this be over? I need it over today. Please, Lord? Let it end. We both need to move on and can't. Her hand rested on her cheek as she turned at Cadee's question.

"I'm sorry, Cadee. What did you ask?"

"Mom and Dad have asked if you might be interested in helping them to set up a community garden at the shelter."

Jaxcy's eyes grew thoughtful. "I would like that. Barnabas has also said that there would be a large garden area here as well. What did he do?"

Guenivere laughed. "It's just Barnabas being Barnabas. He thinks so far ahead of all of us, we can't keep up with him. He has suggested it and has asked, no doubt, if you would like to be in charge?" She continued to laugh at the look on Jaxcy's face. "It won't be all on you, Jaxcy. I can guarantee you that. We will all pitch in. Just think, ladies. We can grow our own veggies."

"And there are to be some fruit trees." Jaxcy sighed, sitting on one of the nearby benches. "That I don't have experience with."

Ennis shook her head as she sat beside her. "Never worry. He'll have found someone to look after that and train us." She studied Jaxcy. "Jaxcy, just how are you feeling?"

"Not great. The medication I was put on doesn't seem to be working. Bruce has found someone else to see me, and that appointment is for early next week. I just wish this was all over with."

"We have been there, Jaxcy. We know what you mean." Guenivere spoke up. "What are your thoughts on who did this?"

"That, I'm not too sure of. There are just so many names."

"Then, let's talk them all over, list the whys and why nots, and see who we can narrow it down to." The ladies laughed as Cadee pulled out a pad of paper and pen from her jacket pocket. "Sorry, this is a habit."

Thirty minutes later, Jaxcy stared at them. "It was him? All along?"

"And her. I don't get it, Jaxcy. Why?" Ennis was upset about her friend.

"I don't know. I want to face them and ask them just that." Jaxcy jumped as she felt a heavy hand on her shoulder and saw the fright on her friends' faces.

"And that you can do, Jaxcy. We have been waiting out here for too long. You will come with us."

Brian Ellsmere stood behind her, his wife, Carol, at his side.

"Brian? You were my friend. Or at least, I thought you were."

He sneered even as his wife gave a cruel laugh. "Never, Jaxcy. Never. We just pretended to be. We had this plan for years."

"Plan? What plan?" Jaxcy was desperate to keep them talking, hoping that some of the fellows would appear. She gave a subtle nod at the look on Ennis' face and knew Ennis was somehow sending out a text.

"A plan to take over a country. Not this one. Who would want that? But there is a nice little island country in the warm ocean. Your parents were on one of the islands in the chain. You and Brennen are headed to one of them. This time, you will not escape us." Carol sneered at the look of fear on Jaxcy's face.

Jaxcy's heart dropped. They had been the ones all along. She had been right. Now, how did she manage to escape and get her friends away as well? It wasn't right, Lord, she thought, that they are here in danger because of me.

"Who wrote the letter to Brennen? We know that Johnny was part of it?"

"Johnny? Oh, yeah, him. He was part of it and then decided that he wanted out." Brian's hand tightened on her shoulder, and she bit back a cry of pain. "We dealt with him."

"What did you do, Brian?" Jaxcy could feel the anger rising in her, anger that was totally unlike her.

She was afraid as well, afraid of what the couple would do to her friends. "Who else is here?"

"No one. Just us." Carol sneered at her.

"No, there has to be someone else. You two would never work on your own." Jaxcy bit back the tears that threatened to fall after the back of Brian's hand slammed across her face. She could hear the distressed sounds from her friends.

"Leave her alone." Ennis spoke up. "How do you expect her to answer you if you beat her." She had caught sight of movement behind the couple and prayed that it was their fellows.

"If you want the same, keep flapping the mouth." Brian's growing rage was showing. His hand gripped Jaxcy's wrist in a cruel grasp and he hauled her to her feet, ignoring her cries of pain and the cries of the other ladies to leave her alone. "You're coming with us, Jaxcy. We really don't care if your man does. He's not the one that we want. You are."

Jaxcy's legs gave way at that point and she collapsed, held upright only by the tight hold that he had on her. Brian began to drag her with him, Carol facing the ladies, a gun pointed at them. She backed up into Brian and then began to curse and shout at him, not seeing the men who had surrounded the area.

Brian's head turned as he desperately sought a way out, and not finding one. He hauled Jaxcy once more to her feet, an arm around her, using her for a shield, even as his own curses were directed at everyone present, including Carol.

Brennen stepped to the forefront, his eyes hard, as he stared at Brian, seeing Jaxcy drooping against the other man, her eyes closed. She was having trouble breathing, that much was obvious.

"Let her go."

"Not a chance. She's coming with us." Brian trained the gun that he had pulled from a holster on his belt and directed it at Brennen. "Get out of our way, all of you."

"I don't think so. This is what you call a stand-off, Ellsmere. You're not getting by anyone of us." Brennen caught a slight movement of Jaxcy's part, as she sagged even harder, pulling the man's arm down and sending him off balance.

"Out of our way." Carol peered around Brian, her own gaze as hard as her husband's, keeping her gun trained on the woman.

No one saw exactly what happened or even knew how Kerry managed to be there. He took a leap towards Brian, his fur glistening in the sun, his hackles raised all the way down his back. The growls that he emitted were loud in the sudden silence. Brian screamed with shock as Kerry latching onto the wrist of his gun hand, dragging it down, forcing him to drop it.

# Chapter 48

Brennen's toes dug into the gravel as he launched himself forward, a fist coming down on the other man's arm. He scooped Jaxcy into his arms and ran, hearing the ladies coming after him. He shot into the lobby of the building, heading for the infirmary, hearing Brady's voice behind him. Running footsteps sounded loud behind him even as he slid to a halt, waiting as Brady shoved open the door and flicked on the lights.

Trying to set Jaxcy down, he found he couldn't. Her arms were tight around his neck, even as she buried her face against his neck, refusing to look up. Brady finally just pointed to the bed and told him to sit and hold his princess.

Barnabas and Dallas found them an hour later, standing in the doorway watching the young couple. Jaxcy had finally moved to sit beside Brennen but refused to let him move away from her. Dallas just shook his head as he approached them.

"Jaxcy? Are you okay?"

She peered at him from under her brows, a dark look on her face. He could see the fear still showing in her eyes.

"About like that, huh?" Dallas sat in the chair that had been moved closer to the bed and watched Brennen, finally nodding. "We have all of the players now, Brennen. Jaxcy. I am sorry that you had to be assaulted and almost kidnapped again.”

“The other ladies?” Jaxcy’s voice was hoarse with her emotions and barely audible.

“They are shaken, have given their statements, and at the moment, are standing right outside the door behind me, waiting to see you.”

“They are? They need to go home.”

Dallas simply grinned. “They won’t.” He shared a look with Brennen and then nodded.

“Who all, Dallas?”

“Who all? That’s a good question.” Dallas pulled out his notebook, Barnabas coming to lean against the foot of the bed. “We have finally solved this, rounded up everyone, and are sorting out the charges. I must say, I have never had a group of criminals trying to put the blame on each other like these ones are.”

“The physician? Was he involved?” Jaxcy felt sorry for the man.

“No, actually, he wasn’t. He was legit. But what you were given has proven difficult to actually determine what the chemicals were. We have finally done that. He is aware of that and that you had reservations about him. Barnabas has spoken to him and agreed to speak with you, to see if you will allow him to continue to treat you, given what I am about to tell you.”

“Mom and Dad?”

"I have a team with them. They are being briefed on the same information that I will share with you. First, your minister? He was part of it, as you have been told. He left a detailed letter in his home down east. He was being blackmailed, forced to pretend to be older than he was. The lady who posed as his wife was not his wife. She was placed in his home to monitor his activities.

"The Ellsmeres were part of it, but not of the upper echelon. They were used to threaten people. He was involved in drug trafficking among other crimes. She was as deeply involved as he was. They saw this as a way to get rich, but they didn't realize that they were considered expendable and would have been killed once they had no value to the group.

"The group? It consisted of members from across Canada. I can't go into details, as it is part of the investigation and charges yet to be laid, but Ellsmere was correct when he said the plan was to take over another country and run it for their own profit. A small island chain was just perfect, or so they thought. There were members who talked too freely and to the wrong, or should we say, the right people and that was how it all began.

"Your parents? They were removed, all within the express purpose of driving you to ask for help from the group. They didn't expect you to survive on your own. They had been monitoring the Foundation fellows. For some reason, Brennen, you were chosen. The minister was forced to write the letter to you. As we suspected, the law was drawn up just to get to you, Jaxcy. They thought that they had succeeded in bringing you under their control when you and Brennen married, planning to blackmail both of you. Why and how? They have never said, and we can't determine. When you left the province, they had to make other plans."

"Is that why they followed us? How does Smithers fit in?"

"Smithers was a low-level criminal, related as we had already learned, to the banker in your home town. The banker is the one who set up the trust fund, forging your parents' signatures to make it look legit."

"Who all from this area was involved?" Brennen shared a look with Barnabas, seeing regret on his friend's face.

"Smithers, the Smothers family, Dale Lewis, the librarian. And then there were a couple of patrol officers, some probation workers, two lawyers, a general practitioner. A pharmacist. A chemist." Dallas paused. "I will let you have names later, but for now, we are still sorting through their charges. Our public relations team is preparing a statement and will be speaking with the press sometime tomorrow or the next day."

"The chemical? How did they do that?" Jaxcy was puzzled.

"The chloroform they used on you, Jaxcy. It was combined with the chemical and there were lesser doses in the cleaner that you were forced to use." Dallas paused, regret on his face. "I am sorry, Jaxcy. I wish that we could have solved this before all that happened."

Jaxcy shrugged, leaning harder against Brennen. "You did your best, Dallas. That's what I prayed, that everyone would do their best. God answered that prayer." She yawned, her ebbing adrenaline playing with her body.

Brennen gave a sound and then slid from the bed, gathering her close.

"If there is anything else, can we talk later? She needs to be resting." He walked away, speaking briefly with his friends and the ladies before he headed for their apartment, finding Jeremiah and Jemma hesitating in the hallway.

Brennen stared at them, realizing that they were all a family now and sighed. He finally had a mother and father that he could get to know. He would always regret that he never knew his own parents, but Jaxcy's parents had taken him into their hearts.

"Mom? Dad? Come on in. I'll get Jaxcy settled and then we can talk." He didn't see the look the couple shared or the tears that sparkled on Jemma's face.

Three months later, Jaxcy straightened up from the garden that she had been working in, rubbing at her lower back. She eyed the long, straight rows of tomato plants, satisfied that they were growing just the way that she wanted them to. She stood and watched some of the ladies who had become friends with her work away, the men from the building around at times. Barnabas had just smiled when she thanked him, for giving her something to do in the outdoors that she loved.

Kerry gave a happy yip and was running from her as she spun, a hand coming up to shade her eyes. A huge smile lit her face and she had dropped her hoe and was running after Kerry, to be swept into Brennen's arm, hugged tightly, and kissed thoroughly.

"You're home, love. I didn't expect you until tomorrow."

"I am home, Princess. And I don't have to travel for months. I spoke with the publisher. He has agreed that I don't have to travel, not unless I choose to and not unless you go with me. It's been a long three days."

"Three days? That was all? It felt like three months." She squirmed in his arms until he set her back down, his arms still loose surrounding her.

"It has. What have you been up to?" He looked past her. "The garden is looking good."

She turned as well, waving at Imly as she walked past her. "It is. The ladies are enjoying it so much. And so are your friends. They are hilarious with their comments, you know."

"I know. And I can only guess that Buckley's are the worst."

Jaxcy began to giggle. "His are. He has already given the garden a date by which he wants to be eating produce. It's far too early. He's doing that on purpose."

"He is. Did they tell you that he gave dates for the weddings for two of our couple friends?"

"They did. They could hardly speak for laughing so hard on how it went back on him."

Brennen shouted with laugher at that. "It was priceless, I must say. I can't wait to meet his lady."

"Me, either." Jaxcy hesitated. "Mom and Dad were around earlier today. They want to head back to our hometown for a bit, just to clear up things, and then resolve whatever it is that they need to."

"It will bring closure for them. Do you want to go along?" He held his breath, waiting for her answer.

"No, I don't need to. I have everything that I want and need right here." She twisted to look up at him. "Now that my lungs are better, and I can do things, I want to explore the area. Will you come with me?"

"I would be delighted to do just that. I know some great hiking trails, places we can camp out overnight. I'll even take you out in a kayak on a beautiful lake up north."

"That sounds delightful." Jaxcy grew quiet, the setting sun reflecting off her face. "Brennen, what would have happened if you had not come to town, if you had ignored the letter?"

"I don't even want to think about that. I'm sure that they would have forced you to marry someone and then you would have disappeared."

"Just like Mom and Dad. They don't talk much about their time."

"No, they won't. They just want to forget it. Listen, how be we head into town? I would like to take my Princess out for a meal."

"I would like that, love. Sorry, Kerry, you can't come. Not this time." She waited for him to move. When he didn't, Jaxcy looked up at him, finding him watching her closely.

"Do you know how much I love you? Do you know how I grieved when you were so close to death? I prayed so hard, Jaxcy. So hard. I really thought God would refuse my request."

"I know, love. You've talked in your sleep." She reached up to kiss him. "We'll set that aside, Brennen. We're not ready to talk that all over. Maybe we will never be." She leaned into him. "One thing that I did learn? We need to be more assertive in our prayers, to be the intercessors that God wants us to be."

"That we do, Princess. When did you get so smart?"

She shrugged, her hand reaching for his to draw him towards the building. "It's just how God teaches me. I study, think, and then learn."

"Never stop learning. You teach me so much as well."

Thank you for choosing the story of Brennen and his Princess, his Jaxcy. Once more, the characters have decided on their own what their adventure would be and how they would learn to trust God through it all. Jaxcy was not the name I had chosen for her. It had been Jemma, which became her mother's name.

How do we pray? Do we pray for our own wants and needs? Or do we spend time in intercessory prayer for our friends, families, and those in need? That is how we need to pray. It is something that I have been relearning as I have written the story of Brennen and his Jaxcy.

Evil is rampant, no matter where you live. Things and events that at one time we would only see in a novel? They have become commonplace. All we can do is trust in God and pray for His protection and strength for our daily walk.

Abe and his team just had to show up again. Their stories are in the *His Guardians* series. Those men and ladies I missed when the series finished. That's why, no doubt, that they show up every once in a while.

And of course, a Shetland Sheepdog, or Sheltie as they are referred to, had to show up. I owned a beautiful blue merle named Noah, his black, gray, white, and tan coat just beautiful. I have two tricoloured Shelties at present, Liam and Natalie.  They add adventure to my life.

God bless each one of you.

Ronna